I AM DIRECTED

The lighter side of the civil service

Augustus Adebayo

Spectrum Books Limited
Ibadan ● Owerri ● Kaduna

Published by
Spectrum Books Limited
Sunshine House
Second Commercial Road
Oluyole Estate
Ibadan, Nigeria

in association with
Safari Books (Export) Ltd
Bel Royal House
Hilgrove Street
St Helier, Jersey
Channel Islands UK

First published 1991

Printed by Johnmof Printers, Ibadan

ISBN 978-246-077-X

Preface

My career has been in the Civil Service. On leaving the University, I entered the Civil Service as an Assistant Secretary and rose rapidly, climbing the rungs of the ladder until I attained the highest position in the State as Head of the Civil Service. I retired voluntarily and entered the academic world in the University of Ibadan and Obafemi Awolowo University, Ile-Ife.

But this book is not an autobiography of my career in the Civil Service. This is a novel, a work of fiction, but built round actual episodes and experiences during my years in the Civil Service. Those who were around in the Western Region of Nigeria and later Western State, will recognise some episodes based on actual occurences. Apart from this, I have indulged, like any novelist, in a flight of imagination. But even when imagination is in full swing, the ingredients for the episodes are founded and based on the principles and practices found in the Civil Service and sometimes on actual experience embelished to produce a good story.

Work in the Civil Service can often be tedious and gruelling; quite often too it can be exciting. But surprisingly, it is sometimes interlaced with hilarious episodes, funny situations and humorous experiences. When people of differing background, education, experience, profession and rank are brought together daily in a large organisation, there is bound to occur every now and again, episodes and experiences that evoke tears of laughter. This book raises the curtain for the reader to see the lighter side of the Civil Service and have a good laugh at an organisation known for its prosaic dullness.

AUGUSTUS ADEBAYO

ONE

There were eleven of us. We each sat nervously and spoke in whispers. The place and atmosphere inspired fear. We were in the Executive Council Chambers where the Ministers meet weekly to decide the fate of the Nation. On the wall, all round us were portraits of former Prime Ministers and Heads of State. Some looked down kindly, some, with fierce moustaches stared straight at you, while two of them glowered menacingly as if they would still come down to deal death and detention on luckless victims of their rule.

As the hour moved to nine o'clock, our eyes focused on the door. The Head of the Civil Service would enter any moment. The thought of meeting such a rare mortal who holds our fate and career in his hands, unnerved some of us. Suddenly, I felt the need to rush to the toilet. I wondered where the toilet could be within the building. Then it occured to me that I might bump on the great mortal on my way out or, worse still, discover that he had arrived and already started speaking by the time I returned to the Chambers. The contemplation of either of these two possibilities made cold perspiration to trickle down my back.

While all these thoughts were passing through my mind, the door suddenly flew open. All of us, as if activated together by some control mechanism, sprang up into attention. A young man sailed in, sporting a large multi-coloured tie which clashed with his blue suit. He approached us rapidly and looked very nervous. He apologised that the meeting was a bit late. He disclosed to us that the Head of the Civil Service was tied up with some urgent state matters. Therefore, he had asked the Permanent Secretary in charge of Civil Service and Establishment matters to come and address us. The said gentleman would be here any moment.

We all sat down again, feeling partly relieved yet still partly nervous. The young man kept pacing up and down looking out frequently through the window. He was ill at ease and appeared even more nervous than we were. Often he would look at our direction, cast a sweeping glance at us and again resume his pacing. We looked at him with envy, someone who was already inside and knew the ropes.

All of a sudden, a voice came through from the outer chamber:

'Tell them to report in my office an hour from now; they are all in trouble.' At the sound of the voice, the young man rushed towards the door and held it open. Presently, a figure appeared, truly impressive with his massive bulk. He had a jolly face out of which two tiny eyes twinkled with undisguised mischief. His head, which had long parted with its hair, shone like marble. But the part of his anatomy which attracted most attention was his stomach. Rising immediately below his chest, it swelled and stretched out for quite some distance, swallowing up his belt and providing bed for his tie which ended mid-way down the stomach. We all stood smartly to attention, each one adjusting his suit and tie.

"Well, well, well, what have we got here?" he boomed out when he came in front of us. "Sit down, sit down. Is every one here?" The young Assistant Secretary confirmed this, fidgeting by his side. "I don't have to tell you who am I; you will soon know, that is, if you stay long enough in the service before you are shown the way out. The Head of Civil Service has directed me to give you a briefing before you meet him for your postings. By the time I finish with you, some of you will regret the day you applied to join the Administrative Service."

He then looked round all of us and started to stroke his tie. "Well, well, where was I" he resumed. "Oh, yes, trying to let you realise that it takes more than a smart suit and bright faces to be an Administrator. I have been asked to address you on the type of jobs you will be performing in the Civil Service and how to go about them. But I am not going to waste my time giving you a lecture. Experience will teach you; for some it will be a pleasant experience but for some it will be a bitter experience. Ask my Assistant Secretary here and he will tell you, even in the short period he has been with us."

At this remark the young man in the blue suit and bright multi-coloured tie laughed nervously, attempting unsuccessfully to be enjoying the joke. During this interlude, the great mogul of the Civil Service had taken a few strides to the window and was gazing out. We were wondering whether he had finished addressing us and his assistant was almost sure that his boss had finished, for we saw him rise and was moving uncertainly towards the door. At this moment, the big boss bounced back to life.

"What are the functions of an Administrator?" he asked, looking round us with an air of great mystery mingled with matchless

2

wisdom.

"How many of you have heard of a word known as POSD-CORB? It is an anagram, a collection of letters which denote the functions of an Administrator. At the risk of delivering a lecture, I will educate you here this morning. 'P' stands for plan; you have to sit down and plan carefully the work to be done and how to carry it out. Even armed robbers sit down and plan careful before they carry out an operation. Has any of you here ever been visited by armed robbers? No one? Lucky you! Lucky you indeed."

With this last remark the civil service god shook his head from side to side several times and seemed to be lost in thought. We guessed that he must have been an unfortunate victim of those night visitors. "Now, where were we? Yes, the next letter is O. This stands for Organising. Not only must you plan what you have to do but also have to organise how you intend to carry out your work. I know you are all great experts at planning and organising how to trap the young ladies in town; those disco sessions and all the drinking and brawling. Let any of you dare lay his hands on our lady typists and he will wish he had never been born." With this threat, he cast a withering look round the room. His Assistant was about to laugh at the joke when he found that the look embraced him as well; the smile which was beginning to materialise, froze on his face.

Oh, Yes, there is the letter S which stands for Staffing. You have to know how to use the staff under you in order to ensure that you get the best out of every member of staff under you. And you do not achieve this by sending them out every time to buy cigarettes for you or to carry secret messages to your girlfriends. At this statement, one of us laughed aloud. "What is so funny, Mr...what is your name? What was the cause of your mirth? "Speak up," cried the lecturer. Our poor friend broke into a voluntary cough and swore that he was not laughing but was seized by a sudden cough. "People who are seized by sudden coughs in the middle of serious discussion are not fit to enter the Administrative class of our Civil Service," concluded the big man.

"Now follows letter D which stands for Directing. As an administrator, you will invariably be directing the whole operation of work entrusted to your section of the department. And when I say directing I mean directing. Once you have planned the work, organised it, you now have to supervise and direct those doing the work to ensure that the way it is done agrees with what is being done, at the appropriate time. Unless you direct properly, you may well find that a journey that should take one day lasts for a whole week and the worse, you find yourself in Calabar instead of Sokoto."

"And that brings us to letter C. Who can hazard a guess what letter C stands for?" The colleague sitting next to me promptly said "Confidential", looking round with a feeling of pride. He was deflated and quickly crumbled when he saw the look on the face of our lecturer-boss. Then another colleague stood up and cautiously said "Conference". By now, the great man could no longer control his anger and contempt. "Good heavens!" he cried, "I never knew I would live to see the day when nincompoops and idiots are admitted into the Administrative Service." Then he walked towards the window and, looking out, he continued to speak in a rather low tone, as if talking to himself. "Gone were the days," he murmured, "when we entered the Service shoulder-to-shoulder with the white colonial officers and we competed with them on equal terms; you just had to be good, very good, in order to survive. Those white boys were efficient, resourceful and very industrious. But we made it, and now what do I see? Twenty years later, I am addressing a bunch of idiots who are to take over from me."

Having given vent to these sorrowful memories, he walked back slowly to us and resumed his lecture in a more sorrowful tone. "Yes, C stands for Co-ordination. As administrators, you should be able to co-ordinate the various activities under you and channel them towards the goal of the organisation." He then looked at his wristwatch and expressed alarm that he had over- spent his time with us. "I am already late for another meeting. Now, where were we? Next letter is R. I knew what answers to expect if I ask you what the letter stands for - Reginah, Rebecca, Ruth, Roseline. Sorry to disappoint you folks, it does not represent any of your loved ones. It stands for Reporting. In any organisation, it is necessary to prepare reports showing the state of affairs, the degree of implementation and execution of work. You need to report on achievements as well as problems and constraints. Such reports will be periodical - monthly, quarterly or annually or as and when the policy-makers call for such reports. You must be prepared and ready to render such reports.

"And now, I must leave you, but we must not forget the final

4

letter B, which stands for Budgeting, and when you talk of budgeting you are really thinking of finance. There can be no administration without finance, and both are, in fact, inseparable. This is because every administrative act has its financial implications. Money is the main measure by which the essential resources of men and materials are allocated for the accomplishment of almost all administrative jobs."

"And now, Gentlemen," cried our big man and moving forward swiftly, he dissolved into smiles as he grabbed our hands one after the other and shook hands. Before we could recover from the surprise he had disappeared through the door, with his Assistant Secretary trailing obediently behind him.

TWO

Before dispersing for the day, we were told that the Head of the Civil Service had invited us to a drinks party later in the day at seven o'clock. We received this piece of news with mixed feelings. One of us who looked as if he was for ever about to cry said "Gentlemen, let me tell you, this is not going to be an ordinary party, it is part of the test to detect those of us who like drinking. Such people will be marked down tonight and they will never earn any promotion."

We all returned to our seats in a state of depression. About three members were in high spirits because they said they had never in their lives drank anything stronger than Coke or Fanta. But their hilarity soon turned sour when another member told them that nobody would believe them and that they would be black- listed as hypocrites. He advised that anyone who drank beer should ask for beer tonight and that such a person would be given credits for being honest. In the end, the result of those contradictory advice and the awful awareness that we were to come face to face with the god of all gods in the Civil Service, threw us all into a state of such anxiety, that we rose and filed out of the room in silence, like mourners returning from the graveyard.

I spent the rest of the afternoon debating what to wear to the party. I should not appear overdressed as to give the impression of a young man already looking too ambitious. At the same time, I should not appear rather shabby as to present myself as a man unfit for high positions. I ruled out a suit and tie. I had only two suits and had worn one during the day; it was the better of the two, newly made for making an impression at the meeting. The other suit was worse for wear, having had it since my student days and carried sundry stains of beer and soup.

The official residence of the Head of the Civil Service was housed on spacious grounds, surrounded by a high fence with an iron gate, behind which a policeman was constantly posted. I approached the gate dressed in a smart native dress. I felt nervous as I did not want to go in too early and find myself face to face alone with the lord of lords and having to think of what to say to him, or how best to conduct a conversation with him. So I decided to hang around the gate until others came. After all, there is safety in numbers.

As I came close to the gate, I discovered that two of my colleagues were already there, lurking behind the gate for the same reason as was agitating my mind. We shook hands and could see that each one was nervous as though preparing to enter an examination hall. We entered through the gate and proceeded to the front lawn, which had been illuminated. There were two tables with a display of assorted drinks and snacks. Four stewards in starched uniforms stood behind the tables. They came forward to ask what we would drink and each of us politely asked for *fanta*.

Within a short space of time, the lawn was packed full. My colleagues and I stood together looking furtively around as various guests came in, roaring with laughter and exchanging jokes. It was easy to see that these were very senior men, long familiar with the surroundings and with the mysteries of officialdom. They were so confident and at ease that I could not help envying them. I also felt a quiet sense of fear of them, for I guessed they must belong to the group at the top, any of whom can crush me with a stroke of the pen.

The party was now getting into full swing with a lot of laughter and back slapping. Each of the members of my group remained motionless. The Head of the Civil Service emerged from the doorway. He was closely followed by two gentlemen, one of whom we quickly recognised as the big man who had given us a talk earlier in the day. He was, as usual, beaming to all and sundry. The second disciple following the Head of the Civil Service was much younger, looking tense and nervous. He quickly stepped forward to pilot the great man to where our group clustered.

Our Chief Host, however, veered off in the opposite direction to greet the lords of the Civil Service who were joking and laughing noisily. Our eyes became riveted on him. Each member of our group quickly adjusted his attire. This highest of all Civil Servants was dressed in white native robes; he was so simply clothed that anyone could have mistaken him for some old rustic uncle from the village, who had come to town to visit his relations. His face was lined but every muscle on it was taut. The most remarkable aspect of his features was indeed his face. The nose descended into a hook, reminding one of those birds of prey like hawk or eagle. On either side of this hooked nose were two bright eyes, sharp and alert and flitting restlessly to and fro, as if picking invisible signals of warning from the air.

He finally approached our group. Once again, there was hurried adjustment of dresses. Each one switched on what each thought must be a charming smile. These same two gentlemen followed him wherever he went; there was the one who was already familiar to us and who looked as old, if not older than the Head of the Civil Service. Then there was the much younger one, who looked so eager to please and wanted to introduce each of us to the big boss, except that he could not recall any of our names. The big boss shook hands with us in turn and later turned to the older of his two satellites and discussed with him for quite some time.

No doubt as a result of the discussion, the big satellite marched to a microphone erected at the centre of the lawn. After smiling sheepishly round the gathering, he cleared his throat several times, and shouted, 'Attention please,' in a voice which made everyone to wonder whatever had brought him into the civil service instead of being a sergeant-major. 'Attention please,' he roared again even when everybody present was silent. "I have the honour and privilege to invite our father and beloved Head of the Civil Service to address this gathering." At the mention of 'our father and beloved Head,' some of the senior men in the gathering exchanged meaningful looks, while a few pinched themselves and one or two actually hissed. Notwithstanding, ever before the speaker finished the last words of his invitation to the beloved Head of the Civil Service he had himself started to clap; everyone joined.

'Our father' walked slowly, even rather painfully, towards the microphone. While my group regarded him with awe, I observed that the faces of the senior men showed different reactions. Some looked at him with admiration, others with distrust and a few gave him a cold look of hatred. "Ladies and Gentlemen", began the Head in a voice hardly audible. "We gathered here this evening to welcome some youngsters into the Civil Service and into the administrative service in particular. I know our professional colleagues in Works, Health, Agriculture will grumble that I do not give these parties when Doctors, Engineers, Agriculturists and so on are recruited into the Civil Service. I am sure you all realise that it is not because I place less value on our professional colleagues, or regard them of less importance in the Civil Service."

Somewhere in the crowd, someone said in an audible whisper 'Really, say that again.' There was a burst of laughter from the area where the voice spoke. The Head continued, "If any proof is required of my high regard for the professions, I only need to remind you that I myself started life as an engineer." Then came another loud whisper, "You turned coat and declared war on us." At this remark which the Head could not have failed to hear, some in the crowd giggled, covering their mouths, while a few threw their heads back and laughed. "Did I hear that some people are planning to declare war on us? We are fully prepared for the enemy," continued the Head of the Civil Service. At this statement, there was a general outburst of laughter in which even members of my group, who had remained tense, joined heartily.

"Now speaking seriously, Ladies and Gentlemen," continued the speaker, "it has become a tradition for us to welcome new entrants into the administrative cadre of our civil service. This is because of the role which administration plays in society. It is not only in the civil service that administrators are needed. There is the work of administration going on constantly in the business world, in the army, the church and in every organisation where human beings decide to organise themselves for a particular purpose. There are also lots of administration going on every hour of the day in the departments of our friends - the doctors and engineers - who are planning to declare war on us." Here there was general laughter accompanied by some clapping.

The Head of Civil Service now surveyed the assembly with a look of triumph on his face. "And now a few words to my young friends who have newly joined the band of administrators in our service. To you, I say, the sky is the limit for those who are industrious, imbued with a sense of dedication and devotion to duty. As for the lazy and disloyal ones, it is part of my duty as Head of the Civil Service to show them the door, quick and fast. Indeed, they will be lucky to take their exit through the door, if I don't throw them out through the window. You will all report in my office tomorrow at nine in the morning, for your postings.

"Now to my colleagues and friends, old war horses and comrades in arms, I say keep on the good work. Our civil service has earned the reputation for efficiency and integrity, not only in this country but beyond. Let us keep it up that way. We are to be seen not heard and we are to observe the triple maxim of impartiality, neutrality and anonymity. We must put our politics in our pockets and carry out the decisions and policy laid down by our political

9

masters. In doing so, however, remember what I have always impressed on you, that you do not have to carry out illegitimate and criminal political demands. We must have the courage to resist these. I thank you all for coming tonight."

With these remarks, the Head turned and walked away slowly into his residence. The party had come to an end. The big fishes started to leave, laughing and talking noisily as they departed. My group still huddled together, but felt greatly relieved. We could now relax. We moved slowly towards the gate and once outside it, we threw our caps into the air and congratulated one another for getting through the ordeal of the evening. No one even took notice whether we drank or not, let alone mark down anyone for what he drank. Some of us now regretted not taking advantage of the free beer.

In order to celebrate the day and congratulate ourselves in our own proper way, we hailed three taxis and drove in a convoy to a popular beer parlour. Now, at last free and relaxed, we started with two bottles each. As we were only seven in the beer club, fourteen bottles appeared, each bathed in cold sweat. We now started to review the various events of the day. "Did you notice that man wearing brown native dress with a white cap? That was the man who came as consultant during our interviews."

"What wicked man!" remarked another colleague. "He was determined to fail me." "Yes," echoed another, "he must have been sent to fail most of us."

"You are being unfair," said someone else who had buried himself in his beer since we sat down and was now well into his second bottle. "You are being very unfair; the name of the man is Mr. Dongo and he was certainly kind and even sympathetic."

"Kind and sympathetic to you," stated the first speaker. "Why not, he is from your part of the country; don't deny it, you are both from the same ethnic group; you are known to be selfish, not wanting to see any other tribe or ethnic group in this country."

The subject of attack sprang up in anger. "Withdraw those remarks or else."

"Or else what?" shouted back his accuser. "The worst you can do is to report me to your big brother and then he can make sure that I never earn any promotion; you can drive me away from your civil service but you cannot drive me away from Nigeria; the country belongs to us all."

"Gentlemen, gentlemen," drawled someone in a thick voice and belching noisily, "You have not even done a day's work in the civil service yet you are talking of promotion."

At this remark, we all burst into laughter, buried our noses in our cups and pulled away at our beer. Wiping his mouth with the edge of his native attire, one of us grumbled, "That Head of Service should be retired; he looks old and tired. Tonight he was talking as though he would collapse any minute."

"Watch it, watch it," whispered one member. "That fellow sleeping near you is from the same town as the Head of Service; this time tomorrow, you will not be lucky enough to be shown the way out, you will be thrown out through the window."

We all turned to look at our friend whose mouth had fallen open and was breathing as if he is climbing a mountain. For the first time we regarded him with envy and hostility. All these days, to have been chatting, sitting and talking with someone who is a town-mate, perhaps a relation of the Head of Civil Service. It was like discovering an enemy within the camp, a cobra snake coiled inside your bed-sheets. For a long time, we looked at the sleeper in silence. Suddenly one of us jumped up and said, "Gentlemen, I am going to steer clear of relatives of the Head of Civil Service." He put on his cap and disappeared into the darkness outside. As if this was an alarm signal everyone who was awake got up and took off home. And so ended the first day of my career as an Administrative Officer in the Civil Service of my country.

THREE

I woke up next morning with a splitting headache. My mouth felt raw and dry. Slowly, I recalled the events of the previous night and how we fled in different directions from the beer parlour. Next, I remember that my group was to meet the Head of the civil Service that morning to hear our postings. What time did he give us? 9 a.m. I looked at my wrist-watch. Five minutes to eight! Good Heavens! I sprang up like one electrified. I had just about an hour to wash, dress and look for transport to get to the Government Secretariat.

We all assembled in the outer office. The Confidential Secretary to the Head of Civil Service ordered two messengers to bring in chairs for us to sit. She was dressed in a smart suit of jacket and skirt, with a red carnation pinned to the jacket. Her face had various shades of colour. The lips were bright red, while the cheeks reminded one of a ripe mango, something between yellow and orange. It was the shade round the eyes that fascinated as well as frightened me. Underneath the eyes and above the eye-lids was a colour of metallic grey, while two rainbows of black line replaced the eyebrows. Altogether, she looked like a painted idol and reminded me of a mended statue, the body is ancient even though the head looks modern.

I was still lost in the contemplation of the amazing spectacle of this lady when a shrill bell rang. I was startled. I looked round to see where the noise came from and discovered the bell high up in a corner of the room. Immediately, the secretary stood up. Her hand went to her bag from which she took out a small mirror. Regarding herself in this little mirror, she touched her hair in different places. Next she took out a strange object and applied it to her lips and immediately those lips glistened with a frightful red brightness.

She picked up a note-book and a pencil, adjusted her dress and once again patted her hair delicately. Then she set herself in motion towards the door leading to the office of the great boss of the civil service. Her process of motion was indeed another amazing spectacle. She practically spinned as she walked, while her back parts gyrated as if dancing to the music of some wild calypso. My colleagues and I watched with mouths agape. The friend sitting next to me pinched me and pointed to the spinning figure disap-

12

pearing behind the door. I angrily shook off his hand for fear that the typists and messengers in the room might see us.

In a moment, the lady re-appeared and asked us to go in to see the Head of the Civil Service. My heart missed a beat. We all rose and moved towards the door, each one exhibiting various signs of nervousness. While some coughed, others hastily adjusted their jackets while one or two tarried behind to allow others to lead the way. The boss was already seated at the head of the conference table in his office. He invited us to sit round the table. We were hardly seated when there was a persistent buzz on his telephone. The boss got up in anger and bellowed to his Secretary that he was not to be disturbed. "But it is the Military Governor who is calling, Sir," pleaded the frightened lady Secretary. "Then why didn't you say so, good-for-nothing Secretary?" "But you did not give me the chance to speak, Sir." Now the great master roared in anger, "Shut up and put me through to the Governor."

"Yes, Sir. Sorry, Sir, I was at a meeting. Yes, Sir. Certainly, Sir. Immediately, Sir. I will, Sir, I will, Sir." These were all we heard in the conversation between him and the Governor. Later, after we had left him we remarked on his servile tone on the telephone, he was even almost putting his hands at the back while speaking. We then gathered that the man holding the post before him lasted only fifteen months when the Governor summarily retired him. Our new boss was only six months on the throne and was at great pains to please the Governor and avert a dreadful fate.

Back with us at his conference table, the Head of Civil Service announced that he had to go to the Military Governor, therefore could only spare a few minutes for us. He opened a folder and read out each one's posting. I was posted to the Ministry of Finance. The Civil Service boss asked each of us to report to his Permanent Secretary immediately. "Any questions?" he said, looking round. "If there are none, then make sure that from henceforth you keep away from my path, unless of course you are posted to this office. Otherwise, if I have cause to send for any of you, then you can very well say your last prayers and sing that ancient sacred vesper, "Now lettest thou thy servant depart in peace." With this, he dismissed us and returned to his desk. We filed out hurriedly, each one trying to beat the other to the door as though the great man would suddenly call one or two of us back and announce that their appointments were withdrawn and cancelled.

FOUR

I made my way directly to the Ministry of Finance and entered the office of the Secretary to the Permanent Secretary. I approached her desk to introduce myself but I could as well have been talking to a table. She was on the telephone, took one look at me, dismissed me with scornful eyes and went on calmly with her conversation: "Me, fifty naira, what does he take me for? Even the girls by the roadside charge more than that these days..." a pause, then "He was trying to be smart, he doesn't know me. I am going to scrape his head and paint it with coal tar..." Another pause, then "I will first ask him to take me to dinner..." Pause, "To his flat after dinner? "No way;" pause, "During the dinner I will look sad and gloomy and tell him that I am owing my landlord three months rent. Besides, I have to attend a wedding next Saturday that I have no money to pay for the shoes and handbag; the two cost 250 Naira. I have only paid a deposit of fifty naira, so that the man will reserve them for me... pause, "what is three hundred? He will cough up five hundred naira before I allow him to touch me..."

At this stage, I could no longer contain myself. Here was I standing foolishly and listening to the amorous campaign plans of a lady, who was not even ashamed of the presence of a stranger. I could waste half the day in this way when I was to have presented myself to the Permanent Secretary. I turned to her and emitted a loud cough to attract her attention. She turned to me with anger in her eyes and I announced, "I am Mr. Alade, the new Assistant Secretary posted to this Ministry by the Head of Civil Service; I would like to present myself to the Permanent Secretary."

This announcement jolted her quite a bit. She put down the telephone in her hand and pressed a button on another telephone, "There is a Mr. Alade here to see you, Sir, he says he is the new Assistant Secretary, Sir." As she spoke, I noticed that she kept her eyes on me, eyes which no longer emitted hostility but an invitation to warm friendship. I said within myself, this slut may be thinking that her prayers for a husband have suddenly been heard this morning with this young man walking in. I gave her a withering look and puffed up my chest to show my defiance of her.

She then turned to me and said that the Permanent Secretary would see me soon, and offered me a seat. Next, she picked up the telephone on which she had been conducting the disgraceful conversation, told the person at the other end that she would ring back as she was very busy. Soon, another buzz sounded on the telephone and "my fair lady" said to me with a charming smile, "you may go in now," giving me a coy look, she patted her hair gently.

I got up and walked to the door of the Permanent Secretary's office and I noticed that my heart started to beat faster while the palms of my hand became moist. I summoned up courage and knocked gently on the door. As I walked in I noticed that the Permanent Secretary had fixed his eyes on me. "Good morning, Sir," I said humbly with a full Germanic bow. The man's eyes twinkled with amusement as he said, "Oh, yes, you are the chap with the funny cap at the party the other night." I smiled nervously while he invited me to sit in one of the chairs before his desk.

"What is the name, again?" "Alade, Sir." "Oh yes. What is your field of specialisation in your degree course?" History Sir," I said beaming with pride. The smile on my face was swiftly wiped off when the Permanent Secretary threw down his pen and shouted "History!" in utter disgust. "Do you think we sit here each day and tell the stories of Napoleon or Hitler and the Great World War? What is the Civil Service coming to when the Head of the Service can send to me a man who knows nothing besides story- telling?" The anger that welled up within him was so much that it left him speechless for some time. We stared at each other, he in anger and I in great fear; fear that if he rejected me I may be told that my appointment was cancelled because there was no other vacancy which I could fill.

After what seemed an interminable length of time he asked "Have you met your U.S.?" "My what , Sir?" I asked utterly bewildered. "Your Under Secretary, he is your immediate boss and you will work up to him, assuming you are capable of any work and not merely trained to tell tales." At this remark, instead of feeling insulted I felt jubilant because it meant I was not being thrown out. He pressed a button on his telephone and asked his Secretary to call the Under Secretary to come immediately. While waiting for the U.S. to arrive, he returned quickly to the papers he was reading when I entered, and appeared completely oblivious of my presence. I spent the interval wondering what this U.S. would be like. Immediately, I started to conjure up the image of a dreadful and forbidding man. I already started to hate him.

There was a knock on the door and the Under Secretary came in. The Permanent Secretary hardly took off his eyes from his papers as he answered the U.S.'s Good Morning greeting. "Yes, good morning; this is your new Assistant Secretary, take him away; put him on Expenditure and switch the other fellow to Revenue." The Under Secretary put his two hands at his back, said "Yes, Sir" with so much servility he virtually ran on the double as he went out of the Permanent Secretary's Office. I followed him, watching the way he was running only on tip-toe and with his two hands at his back. I felt a feeling of pity towards him and I vowed silently within me that I would do my utmost to be friendly with him and make him feel happy in the office.

To my greatest shock and dismay, hardly had the door of the Permanent Secretary's office shut behind us, when the U.S. stopped abruptly in his tracks, squared his shoulders and turned fiercely on me. "Where do you think you are, young man?" he bellowed at me. "How dare you go directly to the Permanent Secretary without seeing me first? Is that the type of protocol you are taught at the University?" I was speechless. The attack was not only unprovoked but it was so sudden and unexpected from a man for whom I was feeling a sense of pity only a moment ago.

And to add insult to injury, I observed that as he was speaking to me he was casting a side glance at the lady Secretary who appeared to be enjoying my misfortune. "Go and wait for me in my office," the Under Secretary said to me. He went straight to the lady with a smile of triumph on his face while the lady started to giggle. I went out of the Secretary's office feeling totally dejected. I found the Under Secretary's office and stood outside the door. I did not want another scene with his secretary. In a moment, the U.S. appeared at the other end of the corridor swaggering in his gait and bullying every clerk he came across. I could hardly believe that this was the same man I saw in the Permanent Secretary's office.

"Go in, go in," he beamed at me. I followed him into his office and on the way, I noticed a scrawny-looking lady in a tiny room, next to the office of the U.S. She looked dry and withered. She too followed us and after delivering a string of messages to her boss, she picked up some files from the Under Secretary's table and went out. I watched her as she made her exit and I could not help noticing that her body seems to lack the centre of gravity, for she walked as

17

though she has suffered a serious dislocation from the waist downwards, reminding one of a crab in motion.

The U.S. asked me to sit. "Now, let me give you your first lesson in the Civil Service. There is what is called protocol. This protocol operates through hierarchy which is a ladder of seniorities. On no account must you deal directly with the Permanent Secretary. I am your immediate boss and you will submit to me all recommendations, advice or comments you may have. You will minute to me in the files and it is for me to decide if the Permanent Secretary should see your submission. You are free to come and talk to me at any time on any matter on your mind. But unless the Permanent Secretary sends for you, you must never venture near his door. And remember, an Assistant Secretary is an egg. Do you know what that means?" I confessed to him my ignorance. "Then let me tell you" he laughed, playing with his tie. "If an egg falls on something what happens to the egg? It breaks of course; and if something falls on an egg, what happens again?" here he laughed loud.

The U.S. then buzzed his telephone and told his Secretary to ask Mr. Kolapo to come. "Mr. Kolapo is the other Assistant Secretary," explained the U.S. He has been on expenditure but the Permanent Secretary has directed that you take over from him." Shortly, the door opened and Mr. Kolapo came in. For the first time since I entered the Ministry in the morning, I felt a sense of relief at seeing someone who is my equal. I felt like jumping up and hugging him but I restrained myself.

"Good Morning, Sir," greeted Kolapo hesitantly, with a look of puzzlement on his face wondering what was the cause of the summons. "Sit down, sit down," said the U.S. with not much enthusiasm. The Under Secretary then went on, "Mr. Alade has just joined us; you will hand over to him and move to the Revenue desk which has been vacant. I think you will need some briefing to set you going. See me first thing in the morning; our revenue prospects are not very bright and you will need to keep a sharp eye on all sources and avenues of revenue." "What is the name again" he said, turning to me. "Alade Sir." "Ah yes, Alade, this means that you are not to pick up your pen and recommend approval of all sorts of expenditure; we are operating on a tight budget. Any questions?"

I was the first to say promptly "None, Sir," because I was eager to get away from an atmosphere which I had found so oppressive since morning. My partner too said "None", and so we marched out and headed for his office. Hardly had we entered his office than I slumped into a chair and broke into a loud laughter. He looked at me with curiosity, wondering what was funny. I could not begin to explain to him my harrowing experience since morning. For me, I was glad to be in a government office where I could for the first time relax without any tension.

I could sense that something was disturbing my partner for he looked upset and angry. Before I could ask him, he exploded. "You better be careful with our U.S.," he exclaimed. "He is a very sly man who loves to take all the credit and put the blame on you; can you believe what he sometimes did? If you sent him a well-reasoned submission which he knew would earn the praise of the Permanent Secretary, he would ask his Secretary to copy it; then he would append his signature, send it to the Permanent Secretary and destroy your own submission. He has done it twice to me. Each time the file came back to me, I found that my own minute was no longer in the file. I can never forgive him. How will the Permanent Secretary ever know of my efforts and ability?"

I looked at my partner with pity and shared his anger. "Why didn't you send your own work direct to the Permanent Secretary when you discovered that the Under Secretary had tampered with it?" I ventured to ask. "And get me kicked out of the Civil Service? Has he not told you about the fate of the egg which gets crushed either way?" my friend groaned. I thought of what I could say to dispel the atmosphere of gloom in the room, for I had had enough of depression and tension and wanted some laughter and gaiety for a change. My friend was the first to speak. "Let us spend the rest of the day together while I hand over to you," he suggested.

I stood up and came near his desk. "These will be your Bibles and you will from now swear by them and put them under your pillow when you go to bed." He held up the Book of Estimates for the year; then the book of General Orders and Financial Instructions. He showed me a file with the title "Treasury Circulars" and explained that they contained guidelines, rules and conditions for the release of funds and management of the budget. All Government Ministries and Departments must constantly comply with them and I must wave the circulars at their face and refuse to budge if they contravene any of the provisions in the circulars.

I must confess that I hardly heard all that my friend was saying for I did not listen. I was so filled with the wonder that the room in which we were talking was my office; to imagine that I now have an office, in a government department and with a desk, a leather-covered chair and two extra chairs for visitors. In a corner stood a filing cabinet. There were even two cups of tea in a tray on top of the cabinet. Was that meant for me too, in case I felt the urge to refresh myself? I felt like jumping up and dancing round the room and before I knew it I was humming:

> Happy days are here again
> Thy sky above us is blue again
> Let us tell the world of it again,
> Happy days are here again.

It was at the sound of my humming that my partner stopped his briefing and looked at me. His look conveyed the curiosity in his mind as to, whether I was being rude, or just being funny, or was some kind of idiot. With a hurt look on his face, he forced himself to smile and said, "If there is any further information you want, I am next door" and he went out.

FIVE

I danced round the room, touching the desk, chair, cabinet, even the door and windows - all mine. My office! Then I went to the chair and sat down behind the desk. My office! I was still revelling in a sensation of delight when the door opened. I turned towards the door and saw a man looking woebegone moving towards me. His face was deep-lined, a long and sad face which made him seem like an ancient kangaroo. He announced himself as my messenger. As I was to learn later, his moody appearance had increased as his compulsory age of retirement drew near. He resented his age and seemed to blame others for it.

At that moment, the only thought which filtered through my mind was the sight of a human being who regarded me with awe. Since I came into the secretariat in the morning, I had been the object of threat and bullying and I was getting used to regard myself as the most lowly creature in government, extremely vulnerable and liable to extinction at any moment. And suddenly here appeared another creature who feared me. My first impulse was to get up and hug him and assure him that we would stand together against all tyranny and oppression. But I quickly restrained and reminded myself of what I had learned in the study of History, that authority is increased by a show of dignity. And so I cleared my throat, said with all the force I could command, "Oh, yes, what is your name?" "Alabi Sir" he answered, attempting a smile which quickly disappeared in the deep furrows lining his forehead.

I sat back in my chair, adjusted my tie, picked up the book of General Orders and Financial Instructions to begin to familiarise myself with the mysteries of government and finance. By the time I looked up, it was getting near to closing time and there was so much still to go through. I got up to look for my partner, Mr. Kolapo. I entered his office and found him adjusting the picture of his wife and his baby which was placed on a small side table. "So you are married," I said with something of a shock. "Yes, what about you?" he answered. "Not for me, thank you," I told him. "Lucky you," he said with rather sad and subdued voice, while I seemed to detect a look of envy on his face. "I came to ask if I am allowed to take home the files and books on my table to study them. I want to familiarise myself as fast as I can with the tools of the trade." My partner advised that I should not take home any files or papers marked secret, but I could take home the books and circulars. He further told me that he preferred to return to the office in the evening to work on his papers and files. I would have loved to do the same but I was still hunting for a flat. This meant an all-afternoon trekking from one area of the city to another, inspecting all sorts and conditions of accommodation, some without toilet, some lacking water and some without electricity. In the end I had to put up with a two-roomed apartment without water or a proper bathroom. It was a far cry from the University undergraduate days when we went on rampage for every little bit of inconvenience.

After supper, consisting of fried plantains purchased from the road-side, washed down with several pints of beer, I settled down in the evening to commence an incursion into the mysteries of bureaucracy. With the accustomed fervour of swotting for university examinations, I attacked the Treasury Circulars, and Financial Instructions and swotted them up till past mid-night. By next morning when I was going to work, I walked with greater confidence and found myself whistling gaily to the office.

On the way, I stopped at a road-side shed for a breakfast of boiled beans garnished with oil and onions. This has been my favourite resort for eating breakfast since I left the University and searching for employment. Now for the first time, I felt a sense of embarrassment. Smartly dressed in tie and suit with a pile of circulars and files, I sat along with mechanics, and apprentice carpenters. I could see that they cast furtive glances at my direction and one of them even nudged the other and whispered something to him. They both looked at me and laughed aloud. I felt uneasy and quickly crammed my food down and dashed out to hail a taxi.

As I entered my office, my messenger with some look of concern informed me that there was a meeting in the Permanent Secretary's office and they had been looking for me. Now my heart nearly jumped into my mouth, or as Shakespeare would put it, my heart started beating at my ribs against the use of nature. In panic, I hurried to the Permanent Secretary's office. As I opened the door, the Permanent Secretary exclaimed "Ha, Alade, here you are at last; this is hardly the way to start a career; now sit down and take notes of the meeting." I sat down nervously and looked round the table. There were two expatriates, my Under Secretary, three Nigerians in suits with serious looking faces, jotting down notes. Facing the

Permanent Secretary was another Nigerian, but in flowing robes and with a cigar in his hand. He kept beaming at everybody round the table. The fingers on his two hands were laden with rings of varying shapes and sizes.

"As I was saying, Mr. Chairman," continued one of the two expatriates, "We still have not agreed on the f.o.b. price. Do you want us to deliver f.o.b. or c.i.f.?" Here panic really seized me. What were they talking about? What is the object of the meeting and what in heaven's name are f.o.b. and c.i.f.? The second expatriate took over. "If we are to purchase cocoa beans from the Marketing Board on the terms you have stated and process them into cocoa butter and chocolates, account must be taken of the issues raised by my partner." Now I knew the purpose of the meeting but what, in goodness name, were the terms stated and the issues raised by the partner? I started to regret ever stopping on the road to eat beans with apprentice carpenters and mechanics. It was in this confused state of mind that the meeting came to a close.

I returned to my office with a feeling of depression. But as luck would have it, the Nigerian in flowing robes at the meeting breezed in shortly after, all laughter and cordiality. "Ah, my son," he laughed, "we have not met before. I am Chief Kensington. I am very keen on this project and I need your help. I can assure you, of good things to come. After all, what is the purpose of your working here? Is it not money you want? I will make you good; you just recommend the project to your Permanent Secretary; I am coming back on Friday and I will arrange good for you."

I hardly listened to all he was saying. My brain was working fast. Here was an opportunity to get this Chief to fill me in on the details of the meeting. I invited him to sit and started by asking the names of those at the meeting. After a lot of effort to get him to concentrate, for he kept on laughing loudly and saying, "I will make you good," I was able to pick out the trend of the discussion at the meeting. This was all I needed to write up the minutes.

It was not quite two weeks after this episode that I encountered a similar and embarrassing situation again. It was another meeting in the office of the Permanent Secretary and I was summoned to be the Secretary for the meeting. This time, I got there before everybody. "Ah, there you are, Alade," said the Permanent Secretary as I entered his office to lay on papers for the meeting. "How are you getting on? Don't hesitate to come to me if you have any problem."

"Thank you, Sir," I said reverently, while inside me I wondered how I could ever summon the courage to go to him to discuss my problems.

The meeting consisted again of expatriates with some Nigerian partners who had come to discuss proposals for entering into partnership for processing oil and bitumen. Officials of the Ministries of Trade and Natural Resources were also present. This time, I quickly passed a paper round for members to write their names and addresses and the interest each one represented. But no sooner had the meeting got off the ground than I found myself lost. There were talks of equity, debenture, preferential shares and much of the discussion appeared to revolve around these esoteric terms. What again in goodness name are these strange terms? I left the meeting feeling depressed again.

I was now convinced that if I was to survive in this Ministry, I must take immediate steps to master the tools of the trade. On leaving the office, I went to look for my colleagues who had read Economics. I borrowed a few books on Banking and Public Finance and on Business, but I discovered to my dismay that they did not possess most of the books which they recommended as compulsory reading. And I had no money to go to the bookshops to purchase them. I therefore directed my footsteps to the library and there, for two or three days a week I swotted up whatever I could to educate myself.

SIX

I picked up the next file from my in-tray, dealing with expenditure matters from the Ministry of Health. On opening the file on the action page, I saw a proposal for capital expenditure amounting to over N2 million for the establishment of Comprehensive Health Centres in the State. The proposal was in a letter addressed by the Permanent Secretary. The Ministry of Health had argued at length in the letter about the advantages of putting up Health Centres in various areas of the State, instead of embarking on the building of hospitals. They had extolled the advantages of the scheme as being a device to save costs and promote cost-effectiveness.

Under the letter, I read a minute written by my Permanent Secretary as follows:

"U.S.; Please invite them to come and discuss; we need more clarification."

Then I read another minute underneath it, addressed by the Under Secretary to me which read:

"A.S.; Above; action accordingly please." I wasted no time in tackling the matter. I drafted a letter for my typist which read:

"Permanent Secretary,
Ministry of Health.

I refer to your letter addressed to this Ministry, on the subject of your proposal to establish Comprehensive Health Centres. I think it will be best if your Ministry comes to discuss this matter in order to clarify some issues. I shall be prepared to have you here for the meeting next Wednesday, at 11 a.m. Please confirm that this time and date is convenient for you."

The letter was soon typed and I signed it, passed it out for dispatch and took my mind off the matter. To my utter amazement, I arrived in the office two days later to find that I had detonated atomic bombs of frightful dimensions. My typist informed me that the Under Secretary had called twice and asked me to report to him immediately. I hurried to his office and the first thing which caught my attention was the file containing the letter which I sent to the Ministry of Health.

"Good Morning, Sir," I said, cautiously approaching him. He did not answer the greetings but looked up at me with cold, steely eyes. "What is the meaning of this?" he barked at me, opening the file at the offending page. "Meaning, Sir?" I stammered, wondering what this was all about, "Did you or did you not write this letter? In whose name and on what authority did you write it?" "But, Sir, you minuted to me to..." "To do what? To write the letter in your name and summon the meeting to your office, to be presided over by you? Oh, Christ!" he barked out again. Now I was speechless.

"Now take the file with you and go and explain yourself to the Permanent Secretary." With this, he threw the file at me, hissed like a venomous snake and dismissed me from his presence. I went out and stood at the corridor, uncertain of what to do next. My mind was in a state of turmoil. Had I reached the premature end of my career in the civil service? Rather than face the ordeal with the Permanent Secretary before being sent packing, why didn't I just throw down the file and disappear? And if I disappeared, I faced starvation in the un-employment market. Now it was my turn to exclaim "Oh, Christ!"

With trembling steps and with my tail between my legs, I headed to the Permanent Secretary's office. Apparently, his Secretary already knew what was afoot because as I entered her office, she started to giggle with a malicious sneer on her face. Without waiting for me to tell her what I came for, she picked up her telephone, buzzed the Permanent Secretary, and told him that I was waiting to see him.

"You are asked to come in," giggling again. I prepared myself for the worst and opened the door cautiously.

"Mister... what did you say your name is again. So, you are the one who has been summoning Permanent Secretaries to appear before you? When are you going to send for me to appear in your office? All this time you have been here, so you have not learned the very first rules in official correspondence?"

"I am sorry, Sir," I ventured to put in, and now for the first time the great boss exploded in anger: "Keep your sorrow to yourself and learn that from henceforth, all correspondence which you sign and issue from this office must begin with "I am directed." Now get out and cancel your letter immediately."

With this I left the Permanent Secretary's office feeling relieved that I had been let off so lightly. His secretary was surprised and disappointed to see me emerge looking cheerful. I blew her a kiss and strode out into the corridor. On getting to my office, I drafted a letter:

"I am directed to cancel my letter Reference No. SP/8/75 of 22nd March. I am further directed to ask you to get in touch with my Permanent Secretary to agree on a date and time for a meeting, to clarify the issues raised in your proposal for establishing Comprehensive Health Centres in the State."

Now in high spirits, I attacked file after file in my in-tray. I came across one file in which my Under Secretary minuted to me as follows:

"Assistant Secretary

Page 47; please direct their attention to the letter and ask for an early reply."

Without wasting any minute, I had drafted a letter as follows

"Permanent Secretary,

Ministry of Works.

I am directed to direct your attention to my letter Ref. No. SP6/88 of 20th February and to ask for an early reply."

SEVEN

Not long after, I found myself in trouble again. It seemed to me as if the Ministry of Finance was specially loaded with pitfalls and potholes to trip the unwary new-comer. This time, it was a letter from the Ministry of Agriculture, asking for a release of the sum of N2.5 million to execute part of their capital projects. I picked up the Book of Estimates and found that over N7 million was budgeted for capital works for the Ministry of Agriculture for the year. I saw no point in refusing to release N2.5 million out of N7 million and so I drafted a letter as follows:-

I am directed to refer to your letter Ref. No. AG/7/MU/68 of 29th April, and I am further directed, to convey approval for the release of N2.5 million as requested in your letter.

A few days later, the Ministry wrote back to ask when to expect the A.I.E. (Authority to Incur Expenditure). The letter came to the notice of my Permanent Secretary. It was his habit to read through all in-coming mail every morning. The Registry would place all in-coming correspondence in a file jacket and send it to him. He would immediately minute his instructions or directive on some of the letters, sometimes in the form of a query. The file jacket would then be passed down to the Under Secretary who would also add his own minutes on some of the correspondence. For example, in some cases where the Permanent Secretary had minuted on a letter.

U.S.
   Please take immediate action,

the Under Secretary would cross out the 'U.S.' and substitute A.S.' which was me. From the Under Secretary, the Mail Jacket would return to the Registry, where the clerks will place the various letters in their appropriate files and send them to the officers who would take action on them.

In this particular case which exploded trouble on me again, my Permanent Secretary had seen in the mail the letter from the Ministry of Agriculture, asking when they should expect to collect the sum of N2.5 million. He minuted under the letter:

Under Secretary;
   What is this all about?
When was N2.5 million approved for the Ministry?

29

Please speak urgently.

The Under Secretary called for the file and discovered that it was I, who had given the approval. He could not contain himself. Instead of sending for me as usual, he burst into my room carrying the offending document. "Now, how do you explain this, my dear all-powerful Permanent Secretary or is it Minister? The sooner you are removed from this Ministry, the better, before you bring down the Ministry if not the government itself."

I was speechless. I was myself boiling with anger. I could not see what I had done to provoke such a vicious attack. He went on, "take the file with you and go and explain yourself to the Permanent Secretary." With this, he stormed out of my office. The thought of facing the Permanent Secretary again unnerved me. I could not summon the courage to face the Permanent Secretary again, or see the malicious leer on the face of his Secretary. I decided to sit tight and await the worst. Each time my door opened or my telephone rang, I nearly jumped out of my seat.

Then the summons came. A crisp voice on the telephone informed me that the Permanent Secretary wanted to see me. I first ran to the toilet. Once again with trepidation, I presented myself before the big boss. "Oh, Yes, Mr...what is the name again?" he began, and then went on, "I gather you wanted to give away a sum of N2.5 million to one Department. I would be most grateful to you if you could tell me where you kept this money, because right now, I am hard put to find money to pay this month's salaries and wages. Where are you keeping this money, Mr... what is the name again?"

"Alade, Sir," I chipped in. "Oh, Yes, Mr. Alade, would you be good enough to come to my rescue and tell me where you kept this huge sum of money?"

Now I was more amused than afraid. "Sir, I checked in the book of Estimates for this year and found that the Ministry of Agriculture had a provision of nearly N7 million for their capital expenditure for this year, and I thought we could..." "You thought... provision... Estimates, you thought..." he roared in anger. I was jolted and startled by the sudden change in his tone. Now he was not jokingly pleading with me to reveal my secret nest of money; he was totally enraged. "Do you have to be taught the most elementary fact that an estimate is merely an estimate of how much we hoped we could raise this year. As the year is just taking off, not much money has yet been collected. As a matter of fact, the

Treasury is at present virtually empty. Do you have to be taught these elementary things? Christ! Go and dish out more millions to other departments." With this, he resumed his reading and I considered the encounter at an end. I hurriedly made my exit. It was only after I had reached my room that I observed a bead of perspiration was gently trickling down my back. But again, I had been lightly let off and I felt quite cheerful.

EIGHT

The Minister had summoned a meeting for 9 a.m. to discuss the financial problems facing the government as a result of adverse economic situation. I had also been summoned to be in attendance to record the proceedings of the meeting. The Permanent Secretary as well as top officials from the key Ministries were present. The Minister opened the meeting by explaining that it had become necessary to re-arrange priorities in view of the downward trend in revenue. Capital projects which had not yet been started should be halted, except projects under foreign technical assistance.

The Minister had just made this opening gambit when we heard a loud disturbance from the Minister's outer office where his Secretary and other assistants worked. The commotion was so loud that it attracted our attention and everyone wondered what was happening. From the outer office came a female voice in angry and menacing tone:

"The Minister is busy at a meeting. What meeting?... Na meeting this baby go chop?... Make I go wait am for house? He don warn me never to come to his house; he say de Madam go shoot me and she go tell the stewards to beat me... Make I go wait am for my house? I don wait and wait for the past ten days, he no fit come. I de hungry, the baby de hungry; na so man give woman belle and no go take care of the woman and the pikin?..."

We were hearing all these clearly and by now the Minister had turned pale. Everyone sat still, too embarrassed to look in the Minister's direction. Then he called me, "Mr. Alade, go and stop that hell of a noise in the Secretary's office."

"Yes, Minister," I responded and went out. I came back shortly after and whispered to him all that he already knew and heard. To my surprise, he displayed the typical politician's knack of getting away with anything. Unembarrassed, he said to me and quite loud enough for everyone in the room to hear, "Mr. Alade, you have not told me anything new; we all heard that. I say, take the young woman away and keep her quiet. If you like, take her; I give her to you free, baby and all." There was laughter round the room.

It was now my turn to be embarrassed. I left the meeting room hastily and on getting to the outer office saw the lady. She stood in defiance of every one, clutching her baby in her arm. I informed

33

her that the Minister had sent me to her and asked her to follow me to my office. She thought it was a trick on my part to lure her away and she announced in a loud voice mixed with anger that she was going to stay put until the Minister answered her. She ended by asking whether Madam, (meaning the Minister's wife) and her children were not being looked after by the Minister. At this, all the junior officials in the outer office began to laugh and giggle.

It was these junior officials who persuaded the young lady to follow me by asking her, how did she know whether the Minister had not sent me to her with lots of money? At this, she followed me and I led the way to my office. As we went along on the corridor I wondered what on earth I was supposed to say to her and how I was to get her off my back, at the same time let the Minister off the hook. If I handled this assignment badly, I might enter the bad books of the Minister and this might adversely affect my career. It was in this state of mind that we entered my office.

I first sought to placate her and win her confidence by playing with her baby. I could not remember when last I ever played with any baby. Taking the child from her, I began to pace the floor, humming some tuneless song. I made a pretence of admiring the baby, even though I could see quite clearly that it resembled a cross breed between a monkey and a goat, with a flat nose, receding forehead and a mouth very much like that of a gorilla. The sight of the baby filled me with disgust.

I had just taken notice that the baby was not wearing any napkin when all of a sudden, a warm liquid overflowed my hands and went down my shirt front and trousers. I hastily returned the baby to her mother, while I struggled to control myself. I was dripping wet with urine. And to add insult to injury, the lady merely took one look at my distress and said, "Which time you will tell me what the Minister say or he no give you money for me and the baby?"

At this juncture, I gave vent to my anger. I stood up from my desk and showed her my wet suit and trousers. To my utter astonishment all she had to say was, "Wetin you de vex for? I think say na baby piss no be animal piss; if he be your own baby, he no go piss for your body? Or you go kill am? I beg, tell me the message from the Minister." I was speechless. I stood for a long while looking at her. For the first time, I looked at her closely to take in her features. A scrawny looking woman, whose breasts had all but disappeared and taken shelter, leaving only two small teats showing underneath a faded blouse. Her eyes were shifty and cunning and her face reminded one of a dangerous serpent ready to strike at an unguarded moment.

I sat down and calmly told her that the Minister had not sent any money through me to her because he was busy at a meeting. I promised to go and see the Minister immediately he was free. I could not return to the meeting for fear that the woman might return there to cause trouble. I therefore stayed in my office to do some work, while keeping an eye on her. Shortly before closing time, I went up to see if the Minister was free and to my surprise, I was told that he had closed and gone home. Now I was completely perplexed as to what to do with the woman and her baby.

I returned to my office and advised her to go home and that I would see the Minister at home and get some money for her. Then came the next bombshell. "Which home I go go? Na this morning I travel come from Bendel State, I no get a single kobo left for chop, not to talk of transport," came the woman's reply. Now I knew I was in trouble. If I advised her to gatecrash at the Minister's house, I would face the wrath of the Minister. And so at closing time, I returned to my bed-sitting room, with a woman and her baby.

The women at the front of the house selling kolanuts, milk, biscuits and other assorted things were surprised to see me return home with a family. I could see them exchanging glances and whispering as we were entering the house. Two of them who were more inquisitive than the others got up and followed us. They opened up a flood of traditional greetings and congratulations to me on the arrival of my wife and baby. One of them even went so far as to say that immediately they saw the baby, they knew it was my carbon copy. I went out and bought some food for my unwanted family.

Later in the afternoon, I made my way to the Minister's residence. Immediately he saw me, he said aloud as though addressing a crowd, "Ah, Yes, Mr. Alade, come in to my study and tell me the result of your meeting today with the technical partners." We entered his study and he now lowered his voice to almost a whisper, "Where is she?" he asked. I told him the story so far. Then he counted two hundred naira to be given to her, with a promise that he would get in touch with her before the month ended. "One thing more, Mr. Alade, thank you. I must remember to put in a word for you with your Head of Civil Service, for quick

promotion. It is such brilliant and cooperative young men like you that we need in the Civil Service."

As I came out of his study, I saw a well-dressed lady who planted herself in my path. I greeted her politely, having no doubt that she must be the Minister's wife. She answered back, "Good afternoon, Mr..." I told her my name. Then another bombshell hit me. "Mr. Alade" she started, "So you have now joined the Minister's agents to carry messages from his girlfriends; I thought you were a civil servant and that you were paid to do government work. Are you also paid to help in breaking people's home? I must speak to your Head of Civil Service. He should tell me if it is part of your official duty to serve as agent in breaking homes."

There are certain incidents in one's life which as long as you breathe and remember anytime, would stay sharply and painfully engraved in one's memory. For me, this moment was one. I stood fidgeting and stammering incoherently before the Minister's wife. She moved forward towards me, with eyes blazing fire. At first, I thought she was approaching to slap me, and I retreated one or two steps backwards. She passed by me, gave me a withering look of hatred and contempt and disappeared into one of the rooms. I made a hurried exit out of the premises.

My eyes were filled with tears, for I was boiling inside with anger and fury. I returned to my flat, threw the money at the woman and told her to get out. Then came yet another bomb-shell. The woman snapped back, "how you think I go get lorry going to Bendel for this evening: All lorries don leave for early morning." Then I asked her where she intended to go and stay for the night. Then came the last straw that broke the camel's back. She retorted quite fiercely, "Wetin wrong for your room here? You no get wife or you forbid sleep with woman? Or abi I no fine enough?" It was at this point that I collapsed on the other chair in the room and I wept with tears rolling down my face. It was faintly that I heard the woman saying, "Wetin wrong with this Oga? Or na crazy man I come follow home?"

NINE

A few days after the nasty incidents of the Minister's wife and the woman with the baby, my messenger dropped a Circular letter in my in-tray and out of curiosity, I picked it up to see what it was all about. My heart missed a beat at the contents. I have been posted to the Ministry of Health with effect from the following Monday. I was to hand over by Friday to a chap coming from the Ministry of Health.

My first reaction at the news was to jump for joy that the Minister's wife would leave me alone once she got to know that I am no longer working for her husband. But then the joy was cut short when I suddenly remembered that I am going to start all over again with a new Permanent Secretary, a new Under Secretary and a new Senior Assistant Secretary; indeed even a new Confidential Secretary to the Permanent Secretary. Those ladies working as Confidential Secretaries to the big guns had a way of wielding subtle power and influence. You could not see the boss without passing through them and their smile or frown could make all the difference to your day; they could encourage and cheer you up with their alluring smiles or completely unnerve and demoralise you with a hostile and cold look. Already I was beginning to be accepted by the crew in the Ministry of Finance and I was feeling at ease with all the top shots and even, with the Confidential Secretary to the Permanent Secretary. Now I was going to start all over again in a new Ministry. Despondency descended over me and I sat glued to my chair, lost in gloomy thoughts.

I spent the rest of the week clearing outstanding work left on my desk and also writing my hand-over notes for my successor. He came in briefly on Friday. We hugged each other. I took from him the cigarette he was smoking and had a few puffs before handling it back to him. We had met at the University in our undergraduate days and since joining the Civil Service, we had met at various meetings. The Administrative cadre is like a cult in the civil service. There is a sense of brotherhood among them, a feeling of common fate and common destiny. Members of the Administrative cadre stick together in defence of their rights and regard themselves as the elites of the civil service. They are meticulous about their dress and it is unheard of to see an administrative officer appear with an open-neck shirt at the office. It is even yet more preposterous to see an administrative officer dressed in incongruous combination, like a blue jacket on a brown shirt and green trousers. By the time a tie is placed on this abominable combination, the brethren of the administrative service will promptly disown such a disgrace to their elite class.

And so we spent most of the morning enjoying each other's company. I asked him if he regretted leaving the Ministry of Health. He had only one regret; he had just started to win the favour of one pretty lady Secretary in the Ministry. Now it is going to be difficult to operate from a distance. "Do you know what?" he beamed at me. "I narrowly escaped a serious danger last week, when bread nearly slipped out of my mouth." "Really, what happened?" I asked. My friend then narrated the story of his adventure. "I went to visit the lady in our office one evening last week. I had hardly settled down when we heard someone greeting the people outside and asking if Remi was in. Immediately, she recognized the voice of her Permanent Secretary. I was frozen on the spot. A cold lump choked my throat. She quickly pushed me towards the bedroom and I ran inside and shut the door. Then the big man entered. I could hear everything going on."

"I hope you did not cough or sneeze," I asked him. "How could I cough or sneeze, when I was covered with sweat? From where I hid, I could hear the big man asking the girl why she was restless and nervous. The girl answered that she never dreamt in her life that a big man like a Permanent Secretary would ever come to see her, and that this was why she felt nervous. Then I heard, "Oh, come on, now what are you nervous about? You are very pretty, you know and I have always been interested in you. Now, I am going on tour next week and I want you to come with me, only for three days." The girl expressed shock and said that if her parents should come to visit her and did not find her, she would be in trouble. Besides, she asked, what would happen to her if Madam should get to know? Our big man replied, "Which Madam? You mean my wife, forget about her. What will she do? Who is going to tell her, you or me?"

"Then the girl played a master stroke," continued my friend. "Let me tell you," he went on, "these girls can be very clever, she told our big man that indeed her mother was sleeping in the bedroom for she was ill and had come to see the doctor." I think this completely put him off for he got up to go. To my delight, he told the girl that he would not like to be coming to see her for people might see him. Then my joy was cut short and I nearly choked with anger when he added that he had a room permanently reserved for him at Primrose Hotel and asked the girl to go there the following evening. She should go straight to Room 507 on the fifth floor. The girl said she could not leave her sick mother alone, besides if her father should get to know that she has started to living that sort of life, he would kill her. Our big man laughed heartily and said, "before it was Madam, now it is your father." When I heard the girl protesting "No, Sir, No, Sir, leave me, Sir," I could sense that he was attempting to grab her. My blood boiled up within me and I clenched my fist in anger."

On hearing this, I laughed so much that my ribs were aching. I asked him why he had not come out of the bedroom and punch the boss on the nose. He retorted, "Thank you, would I be here this morning to take over from you?" "Why not?" I answered, "it would be madness and even mad people know when to play it cool."

Then we changed the topic and he asked me about life in the Ministry of Finance. I briefly recounted my experiences and I narrated my encounter with the Minister's wife. To my surprise, my friend warmed up to the subject. "Oh, you have lost a good chance to make life comfortable for yourself. That woman would have heaped money and clothes on you and would have put pressure on all who mattered to give you a fast promotion." "What do you mean?" I asked, for I was really puzzled. "Can't you see that a woman like that, whose husband is running after so many women, must be lonely and yearning for someone to comfort her."

"And how do I fit into the picture?" I asked. "Easy and simple," answered my friend. "You think I earn the name Chief Planner and Strategist for nothing? Now listen; I saw the woman at the party for Independence celebrations standing alone in the crowd while the Minister was bouncing from one group to another. I could see right away that there was a sex - hungry woman; it showed in her eyes."

"Really, how do you read sex hunger in people's eyes?" I asked.

"Easy and simple, I know six ways by which you can pick out such women. The first one is, if you see a lady at a party whose eyes rove round the young men at the gathering and keep looking at the bulge in their trousers, then go straight for her, you cannot mistake her."

"And then earn myself a dirty slap," I said, laughing.

"No, I assure you, use this your Minister's wife as a test case. Go to the house when the Minister is away and say that you come to apologise and to assure her that you did not support the Minister's escapades. As you are talking, keep rubbing the front of your trousers. You will see that her eyes will be fixed on it, and before you know it, she will drag you inside and tear down your pants."

"And suppose the Minister comes in suddenly and catches me with his wife?" I queried.

"Why are you so naive? Leave that to the woman. Women know a hundred and one ways to handle such situations. You will leave the house whistling away and she will beg you to promise her that you will come regularly to service her."

"And what if I don't ever attempt to see her again?"

"Whether you hide in hell, she will come and fetch you there. She does not want your money; all she needs is that you come and pound her regularly and give her all the afternoon delights she has missed. Half the money the husband has stolen will come into your pocket and you will become wealthy for ever after. Please, do not forget me when you come into your kingdom."

With this, we both laughed and then suddenly, we noticed that the messengers were beginning to shut the windows. We both looked at the time and discovered that the day had ended. I hurriedly thrust my hand-over notes in his hands and we picked our coats and walked out of the office.

TEN

I entered the Ministry of Health the following Monday with some trepidation. A bit nervous in case I would go through another initial nasty experience such as I had in the Ministry of Finance. I had learned not to jump the gun but obey the rules of hierarchy. I therefore reported to the Senior Assistant Secretary. On entering his office, I found four Nurses in white starched uniforms with little bonnets on their heads. Two of them were skinny with spider legs, while the other two were large breasted and seemed as if they would burst out of their uniforms at any moment.

As I opened the door, all heads turned and looked at me. From the look on the faces of the nurses, and the smug look of pleasure on the face of the Senior Assistant Secretary, it was obvious that the nurses had been coaxing and flattering the S.A.S. for some official favour. I approached the desk and greeted the S.A.S. politely and nodded to the ladies in uniform. To my delightful surprise, the S.A.S. greeted me with expansive friendliness, "Ladies, meet Mr. Alade, our new Assistant Secretary." Then turning to me, "You came at the right moment because this matter is on your schedule; the ladies have applied to go on overseas courses and you will have to process their applications."

Once again, the ladies all turned to look at me, this time regarding me with greater attention and respect. I even sensed two of them devouring me hungrily with their eyes. I was at a loss as to how to react to the situation, and so I found myself smiling sheepishly back. Half of my attention was working on the challenge from the eyes of the two ladies, while my remaining attention remained correctly official on the subject of the ladies overseas application. The S.A.S. went on, "I believe your colleague was with you last Friday to take over from you; this morning, he will be waiting to hand over to you before moving to the Ministry of Finance. So you had better go along and join him, then see me when you have settled down later in the day." With this, I left him with the nurses and went to look for my new office.

I traced my new office on the first floor and found my colleague already waiting. "Sonny Alade, my boy, have you made the first assault on the Minister's wife? I will take it as part of your handing-over to me and I will seize the earliest opportunity to make her

'Avoid those women like plague, they are hungry for husbands... they will suck you dry, hollow and throw away your carcass.'

the happiest woman in the world." "You are welcome to her and to the Minister and the entire household," I answered. "Now, Sonny, don't be so sarcastic," he sneered back.

I collected his hand-over notes and was about to bid him good-bye when the four nurses whom I had seen earlier on in the Senior Assistant Secretary's office walked in. My friend knew them well, as I could observe from the familiar greetings. He introduced each of them to me by their names. The nurses apologised for intruding at such an awkward time and promised to call back again when I am more settled. They implored me to give early consideration to their application.

When they had gone, my colleague turned to me and said in low tones, "avoid those women like plague; they are hungry for husbands and if you allow them to hook in on you, then you have had it; they will suck you dry and hollow and throw away your carcass." I was puzzled because I heard him introduce three of them as 'Mrs', and I told him so. He laughed out heartily. "Na lie; they use "Mrs" to hide their shame and embarrassment. Three of them were married but their husbands disappeared when they discovered these were not women but wolves in sheep's clothes. So keep away from them."

"How do you come to know so much about them?" I asked him. "Never mind that, and let me tell you one more thing about them; those swellings which you see on their chest underneath their uniforms are not real breasts."

"Not real breasts? What else can they be?" I wondered.

"Sonny boy, you have a lot to learn; they are pieces of cloth and rags tucked inside their bras." The very thought filled me with disgust but before I had time to express my reaction, my colleague breezed out to commence a new lease of life in the Ministry of Finance.

I now sat back to digest my new schedule of duties. Hardly had I read more than two pages when a gentleman walked in. I looked up and saw a figure standing like a scare-crow. He was extremely tall, but so thin that I wondered if he could be really flesh and blood. To add to the curiosity of his appearance, there was a whole forest of whiskers mounted on his upper lips, the hairs sprouting wildly in different directions. But for the fact that he was decently dressed in a fine suit and spoke in refined English, I would have mistaken him for an apparition and scream for help.

"I believe you are Mr. Alade, our new Assistant Secretary; I am Dr. Folarin, Chief Medical Officer. Did your predecessor mention to you a matter about a man who is taking us to court over his contract for the supply of drugs? I have just checked upstairs and I was informed that you have been instructed to take certain actions."

Now, this man continued to give me fresh cause of surprise. When he spoke, his voice rumbled like peals of thunder, deep and re-vibrating. For á moment, I just stared at him in wonder, for I could not imagine how a man with hardly anything to call a chest could produce such a sound.

Without waiting for me to reply, he emphasised that the matter was urgent and I should let him know the position before the end of the day. My immediate reaction is to wonder how many bosses I was supposed to have in the new Ministry. I had met the Senior Assistant Secretary only briefly. I was yet to meet the Under Secretary, not to talk of the Permanent Secretary, the little god of the Ministry.

For the meantime, I directed my attention to the file dealing with the matter of the contractor who had threatened to take the Government to court. After having gone through the papers, I was in no doubt that the man had no case. All the delays, the loss of his equipment on the building site and other misfortunes have been caused by his own negligence and lack of attention to details. How could he turn round and blame government? Now he was claiming over two million naira as compensation over the building of a hospital and supply of equipment.

The Under Secretary had minuted in the file that the matter be referred to the Government's lawyers in the Ministry of Justice for advice. As far as I was concerned, the matter was simple and straightforward and I saw no need to refer it to the Ministry of Justice for advice. I therefore picked up my pen and wrote a minute as follows:

> "Permanent Secretary,
> Via Under Secretary,
> Via Senior Assistant Secretary.
>> I refer to the minute at page 83 in this file,
>> instructing me to refer the matter of Alpha
>> Company and Co to the Ministry of Justice for
>> advice. I think this is a simple case, and the law

46

on it is clear. It falls under what is known in
Law as <u>Non Voluntas Injurias</u>; the contractor
has failed to demonstrate sufficient diligence in
his handling of the contract and he is therefore
guilty of what the law knows as <u>negligentia</u> or
<u>culpa</u>. Subject to your approval, I have written
at page 87 to inform the Contractor accordingly."

I had just settled in my office the next morning when tons of
bricks and fire-works descended on me. Promptly came the message that the Permanent Secretary asked me to report in his office
immediately. My heart nearly jumped into my mouth. What again
have I done in my new Ministry? Ordinarily, a Permanent Secretary hardly has any cause to send for an Assistant Secretary.
Whatever information, directives or questions he may have will
be directed at his Deputy or the Under Secretary or the Senior
Assistant Secretary. It is from these little gods that the Assistant
Secretary takes his cue.

What can the matter be now? I kept repeating this thought to
myself as I went up the stairs and along the corridors. As I entered
the Permanent Secretary's office, the first thing which I noticed was
that all the little gods were standing in front of his desk. Immediately, I started to relax, thinking there must be a staff meeting of all
his administrative officers. As I said, "Good Morning Sir," the
reaction which I got showed that I was in serious trouble.

"Are you sure this is a good morning, Mr... what do you call
yourself? Who do you think you are and where do you think you
are?" The little gods standing round were looking at me as one
would view some revolting and detestable specimen of nature.
What, in heavens name, had I done wrong again and why should
trouble and misfortune be dogging my footsteps everywhere I go?
These were the immediate thoughts that filled my mind as I stood
nervously before four pairs of hostile eyes.

Then the Permanent Secretary resumed the inquisition. "What
did you read at the University?"

"History, Sir," I answered.

"You then went on to read Law for your second degree?"

"No sir."

"Ooh, at what stage did you do your Law degree and presum-
ably called to the Bar?"

"I have never read for any examination in Law, Sir."

Then he sat still and fixed his gaze on me for what seemed to be almost an eternity. "Mr Oni," said the Permanent Secretary, turning to his Deputy, "take this fellow away before I explode; he should withdraw his mad letter today and show it to you."

With this, I was led out like a sheep for the slaughter by three angry-looking men. The Deputy Permanent Secretary instructed the Under Secretary to handle the matter, and so I followed the U.S. to his office. There, I was given a thorough dressing down.

"Look here," began the Under Secretary, "no matter whether you took a doctorate degree in Law, whether you are Professor of Law or a Senior Advocate of Nigeria, so long as you are employed as an Administrative Officer in the Civil Service, you are not qualified or competent to advise government on matters of law or make any pronouncement on legal matters. That responsibility belongs to the Ministry of Justice. Now, go and withdraw the letter which you sent to the Contractor and refer the whole matter to the Ministry of Justice; impress on them that it is very urgent."

With this, I left the Under Secretary's office. For the rest of the day, I was crest-fallen, for the first time, I started to envy those who are self-employed and are their own masters.

ELEVEN

Preparations were being made for the opening of three rural hospitals in the state. I was assigned the task of ensuring the smooth-running of the opening ceremony in each place and ensuring that everything went well without any hitch.

Now I was in high spirits. A few days before, I had visited each of the three towns in which the hospitals were built. I had gone to the sites and inspected the preparations. In each town, I visited the Head Chief in his palace and briefed him and his chiefs in preparation for the opening ceremony in the town. I felt truly elated. Here was I, dashing round from town to town in a government vehicle, inspecting sites and addressing chiefs. I blessed the day that I was posted to the Ministry of Health. It is a far cry from the Ministry of Finance, where there was nowhere to visit and you spent each day shut up in your little cubicle of an office.

On return to the office after one of my trips, I observed that one or two circulars and some leaflets had been deposited in my in-tray, together with a few files. I told myself that everything in that tray would have to wait until after the opening ceremonies of the hospitals. I ignored all papers on my desk and jumped out gleefully every morning to tour the various centres for the opening of the new hospitals.

The day finally came, for the opening ceremony of the first hospital. I had alerted the Head Chief and advised him to mobilise all his people to the site. To make the occasion colourful, I had urged them to bring their native drums, musicians and dancers. That morning, I did not even bother to reach the office. I went straight from my house to the village. On getting there, I went directly to the Palace and roused the Head Chief and all his people. The Head Chief and I led the procession of dancers and musicians to the site of the ceremony where a pavilion had been erected, with gaily adorned banners.

I felt really good. For the first time in my life, I felt a sense of importance. Until the Minister and the Permanent Secretary and other important official dignitaries would arrive an hour later; I was for the moment, the representative of government; the government which had brought a great blessing and happiness to the town. And so I was idolised, the drummers crowded round me and sang my praises and the ladies of the town, bedecked in their jewellery and colourful dresses, placed a garland round my neck. One of them thrust a horse-tail in my hand and I danced a few steps to the jubilation and applause of all the crowd.

The townspeople sat down, the Head Chief, sat in his apportioned place next to the seat assigned for the Minister. His chiefs and other local dignitaries sat in the second row, because all the seats in the front row were reserved for the Minister and all the top officials coming from the Ministry. Until the Minister would arrive, I took the liberty to sit down on his chair, next to the Head Chief. The drummers and dancers continued to entertain the gathering.

An hour passed and there was no sign of anyone from the Ministry. Another half hour went by, and yet no one appeared. Then another hour, and still no sign of the Minister or any officials. The Head Chief had started to sweat under the weight of his heavy dresses and regalia. I was becoming nervous. I got up from the Minister's seat and walked away some distance towards the road leading to the town. I was hoping silently that I would see the Minister and his entourage driving up the road, with profuse apologies for their being late. But there was not a single soul in the distance.

Now I was beginning to worry. What could have happened? Could the ceremony have been cancelled or postponed at the last minute? Such postponement could only have been decided that morning because I was in the office throughout the previous day and no 'such announcement had been made. As I walked back towards the gathering, I could sense a feeling of uneasiness. Even the dancers and drummers had packed up and taken shelter. All eyes were turned in my direction. I walked unsteadily towards the Head Chief. The local elites got up from their seats and came towards me. The question on every lip was uttered in unison: "What is happening?" I looked stupid and stammered incoherently.

By now, everyone in the gathering had stood up; a few were walking away, quite a number joined the little crowd which had surrounded me. Many were heard saying, that they had always known that no one could trust government. Some boldly shouted that it was a government of rogues and liars; when the government knew that it had no money to run the hospital, why was it deceiving the people that it wanted to open it? One or two intrepid folk

50

shouted at me that I should go back and tell my government of rogues and liars that they should never dare to show their faces in the town.

Amidst the confusion and turmoil, I made a hurried exit. On reaching the office, I was informed that the Senior Assistant Secretary had asked for me. I was puzzled; asked for me when he and the others should have been at Ibese town for the day's ceremony? Then I asked a colleague in the next room what was happening. He regarded me with curious surprise. Did I not see the Circular sent out the previous week postponing the ceremonies in the three places?

I hurried back into my room and rummaged through the in-tray on my desk. And there, lo and behold was the Circular. Indeed, in addition to the Circular, there was a note from the Under Secretary, asking me to inform all the communities concerned of the postponement. Cold perspiration broke out on my forehead. I had not bothered to look at the papers on my desk for over a week. The climax came the next day when I looked through the window in my office and saw the Head Chief of yesterday and a few of his people. I sent out my messenger to find out what they wanted. I learnt that the delegation had come to see the Minister, to find out the cause of the previous day's fiasco. I could not bear to face what would undoubtedly be another unpleasant experience for me.

I told my colleague next door that I was not feeling well and that I was going to the hospital, in case the bosses upstairs asked for me. With this, I bolted and disappeared from office for the rest of the day.

51

TWELVE

Preparations were nearly concluded for the National Conference on Health taking place in Lagos. It is a Conference of all the Ministers of Health throughout the Federation of Nigeria. They were accompanied by their officials and advisers. My Permanent Secretary directed me to come along to service our delegation. As Assistant Secretary, my duty will be to see to the booking of accommodation in the hotel, to pay for all expenses of the delegation and to arrange for transport for every member of the delegation. I would be responsible for ensuring that all the papers for the conference were in order and that every member is with his own copies. Above all, I would be on call to run sundry errands for the delegation.

The Minister said that he would leave very early for Lagos a day before the Conference was due to start. I was directed to get all the conference papers and the briefs, which were being prepared in the Ministry to reach the Minister at his residence not later than six o'clock in the morning of the day he was due to leave for Lagos.

I woke up shortly after five o'clock in the morning, collected all the Minister's papers and set out for his residence. As I entered the premises, I heard what sounded like a commotion from inside the house. As I drew nearer the house, the noise grew louder and I wondered what could produce such a violent quarrel so early in the morning. It was not yet six o'clock.

I entered the house and to my great amazement, I noticed everyone kneeling down for the prayer being said by the Minister in such a loud voice as if he was engaged in a brawl. He was shouting at the top of his voice and with menacing gestures. I came in on tiptoe and bowed my head to join in the family devotion, if such a scene could be described as a devotion.

My amazement became greater as I listened to the Minister addressing the Almighty. "Oh God, for over a year I have pleaded with Mama Toyin, my wife, to allow Gloria, my junior wife, to come home. She had bluntly refused and threatened to cause trouble for me if I bring in Gloria. Oh God, make Mama Toyin see reason, let her realise that it is in her own interest to allow Gloria to join me." And then he went on, "Oh, God, if after all persuasion, Mama Toyin still refuses to allow Gloria to come in, then Mama

Toyin herself will have to leave this house; she will pack her things and get out. It is then that starvation and suffering will bring her to her senses. I will not support her with a single kobo."

It was at this juncture that the Minister's wife, who was kneeling beside him and who obviously must be Mama Toyin, got up and went to sit on a near-by chair where she started to hiss vehemently like a venomous snake. Soon, the prayers came to an end after a chorus of the Lord's prayer which the Minister intoned in a voice much louder than the main prayer.

On getting up, the Minister saw me. I greeted him and to my great bewilderment he asked, "Mr. Alade, it is good to see you; what brings you here so early in the morning?" I then reminded him that he had instructed the Ministry to deliver his conference papers very early that morning. "Conference, what conference?" he asked. I looked at him with great astonishment. Summoning all the self control I could master, I reminded him about the National conference in Lagos and the fact that he asked for his papers early that morning because he intended to leave for Lagos.

Now amazement continued to increase by the way the Minister reacted. "All these useless conferences," he exclaimed, "what is their use? I get nothing from them except a lot of grammar. I know how much my colleagues in the Ministries of Finance, Industry and so on make regularly. All that you people do in the Ministry is to send me plenty of papers and memoranda to read. Put the papers on the stool there." With this outburst, he turned away from me and appeared to be completely oblivious to my presence. After hanging around for a few minutes, I left his residence. It took me quite some time to recover from the successive surprises and shocks which I experienced in the Minister's house.

The National conference opened in Lagos. The chairman, who was the Federal Minister of Health was a man of gargantuan dimensions. His neck had virtually disappeared within circles of fat which secreted continuous sweat which he perpetually wiped with a large piece of cloth, much too large to be described as an handkerchief. The few strands of hair on the edges of his bald head were laced with white hair. His ears were over-large and even flappy. Deep facial wrinkles shot down from each end of his flat nose, passing his mouth on either side to fall beyond his chin and lose themselves in the mass of fat around the neck.

The meeting was now called to order for the commencement of

the day's proceedings. But my Minister was nowhere to be found. Our delegation became perplexed. Where was he? He was supposed to have left for Lagos the previous day. Just as the Chairman was completing his introductory remarks, my Minister breezed in, looking very distraught. His hair was unkempt and he looked as though he had been engaged in a brawl the whole night.

He spent the next few minutes arranging and re-arranging his papers; I noticed that some were upside down. When the Chairman announced the first memorandum on the agenda, my Minister turned round to our Permanent Secretary and exploded in anger that the memorandum under discussion was missing from his papers. The Permanent Secretary gave me an accusing look and I hurried to the Minister. I took the folder containing his papers and there, amidst personal letters, bills, survey plan, cement contract, I fished out the memorandum and handed it to him.

By the end of the day it became necessary to prepare additional briefs for the next day. The Permanent Secretary asked the Chief Medical Officer to head our team and prepare the briefs. On reaching our hotel, the Chief Medical Officer summoned a meeting, and there he started to give me assignments which I must complete and submit to him before the next morning. I resented a Medical doctor having the audacity to give me instructions. I was an Administrative Officer, the elite corps of the Civil Service and how dare a medical doctor to order me around. I politely declined to carry out the assignment on the excuse that the Permanent Secretary or the Minister might require me at any moment for urgent assignments.

Now the Chief Medical Officer, a thin man with voice like thunder, boomed out in anger, "But what is wrong with all these Administrative officers? Look at this boy refusing to carry out my instructions. What makes you the Administrative Officers think that you are superior to all other people in the Civil Service?" I answered back, "I have not talked of superiority; I merely said that I might have other urgent assignments."

"Shut up," he boomed. "You are all the same. I was already a medical doctor before your Permanent Secretary ever dreamt of entering a University; you must be an infant when I had been practising as a doctor. Now the Permanent Secretary is the boss of everyone. Someone has got to tell the government that if this unjust and ridiculous situation is allowed to persist, it will be the ruin of the Civil Service and of government itself." He had got up from his chair and started to pace up and down, while the medical doctors under him, who were in the room regarded him with awe and spoke to one another in hushed whisper. I was merely amused, knowing fully well that he would never write my confidential report and had nothing to do with my promotion.

As the conference was to resume at ten o'clock the next morning, it had been agreed that our delegation would assemble at the Minister's place an hour before in order to brief him for the day's work. With some effort, the Minister dragged himself out of the bedroom, his eyes were blood-shot and he kept yawning dismally while regarding us with silent hostility. It was obvious that he badly needed some hours of sleep. The Permanent Secretary opened the discussion with some preliminary remarks, then called on the Chief Medical Officer to expatiate on the details of the proposals in the memoranda for the day.

The Chief Medical officer's reaction caught everyone with surprise. "Why me, now" he began, "I thought you bright administrative boys are supposed to be all-knowing and to have answers to every thing, go ahead and brief the Minister." My Permanent Secretary was jolted by this unexpected turn of events. He said "If I may ask, what may be the cause for this unwarranted out-burst, C.M.O.?" Now the C.M.O. could no longer contain himself, "Unwarranted, did you say, P.S.? Ask your insolent rat there (pointing to me). Your administrative boys will be the ruin of the Civil Service and of the country. I have been practising medicine before you ever entered the University..." The Permanent Secretary took it all very calmly. He said in a cool voice, "Whatever Mr. Alade might have said or done to you, surely you have no right to refer to him as an insolent rat. You owe the young man an apology."

"Apologies my foot," boomed out the C.M.O. "You and all your administrative bright-eyed boys will wait till doomsday to get an apology. We professional people are treated with disrespect and even contempt in Government service."

Now the Minister was fully awake and alert looking from one speaker to another, partly in alarm and partly in amusement. He intervened. "I don't understand the reason for this early morning quarrel. I shall have to mention this incident to your Head of Civil Service. With the present mood, I do not see how we can have any meaningful meeting now." He had hardly finished saying this

56

when the Chief Medical officer got up and walked out followed by his medical lieutenants. The meeting came to an abrupt end. The Permanent Secretary was as cool and suave as ever. He was starting to apologise to the Minister for the ugly incident, when the Minister got up and disappeared back into the bedroom, no doubt very happy at the turn of events.

THIRTEEN

I turned up at the office one morning to find an official circular letter with the heading, 'POSTINGS'. The fact that it was sent to me meant that the postings affected me. I quickly ran my eyes down the list of names and there was my name - R.A. Alade from the Ministry of Health, to the Premier's Office. My heart missed a beat. I had always regarded with awe the people who worked directly in the Premier's office. They knew all the top secrets and latest developments in government, and they went around with an air of self-importance and superiority.

One of my duties was to over-see Parliament and all matters connected with it. There were gadgets that needed repairs or replacement, catering arrangements for refreshments, administration of the junior staff working in the Parliament buildings - clerks, typists, gardeners and drivers.

Of all the assignments in my various schedules of duties since I joined the Civil Service, I found this one the most pleasant. It gave me the opportunity of getting out every now and again to go to the Parliament buildings. Quite often, there was nothing in particular for me to do. I would stroll round the premises, bully one or two gardeners and end up at the catering kiosk where the girls there were only too anxious to please me with cake washed down with a cup or two of tea, and all on the house!

I soon discovered that the junior workers at the parliament buildings did not take kindly to my frequent visits. Some were either lying on their backs and sleeping while some had disappeared for the day to run their little business in town. I constituted a constant source of nuisance by the queries which I issued to them with the threat of termination of appointment. Very soon, they devised a way of alerting themselves whenever I appeared at a distance. Whoever spotted me first would shout 'Ra- a-a-a-'. I presumed this stood for my initials R.A.A. Once the signal went up, those sleeping would jump up and go for their cutlasses, while those engaged in playing pools would crumple the paper in their pockets.

When Parliament was in session, it was part of my duties to attend and hold a watching brief for the Department. Parliament had areas reserved for the Press, Visitors, Officials where they

could sit and watch the proceedings. Then came this fateful day, a day of drama when all hell broke loose in the Parliament. It was like watching a horror film, something entirely out of this world. But first, let me briefly narrate what led to the horror.

There was internal friction among members of the ruling party. The friction finally broke into open conflict, in which one faction supported one leader, while the other faction supported another leader, as Premier. Suddenly, there were two Premiers in the House, sitting and facing each other with their supporters behind them. Sticks and cudgels were hidden underneath voluminous robes. The signal for pandemonium sounded, when the Speaker attempted to rule in favour of one faction against the other.

All of a sudden, one member rose from his seat, rushed forward to where the Mace, the symbol of authority of the house, rested, picked it up and broke it into two. Then members rose from their seats and set upon one another with fists and cudgels. The old and the infirm, who had no stomach for such an encounter made for the windows to climb out, since the door-way had been blocked. I suddenly noticed my former Minister of Health hauling his bulk against the window but could not scale through. He landed on his back as the foe came upon him to deal blows on his head. "I take God beg you," he shouted on the ground, "you know I have no hand in all this." His foe put a foot on his chest and said, "Shout clearly that you will never again oppose us; do you call that shouting? I cannot hear you." All the while the Minister could only babble. "I beg you; have mercy on me. From today, I am for you."

My attention shifted to another scene in the arena. One of the two Premiers stood his ground, perhaps out of dignity. When his assailant came upon him, he immobilised him by the simple process of wrapping his voluminous robe round the head of the assailant, which left him helpless and struggling for air and vision. Now pandemonium really ensued. It was a scene of horror, as men running for safety were pulled back, while a few abandoned their resplendent robes and fled helter skelter looking for an opening to escape.

Amidst all this scene of carnage and savagery, the person I wanted most to receive a few severe blows was my erstwhile Minister of Finance, who had given me some unpleasant experiences when I was in his Ministry. My eyes roved around the battlefield; he was nowhere to be found and I had not seen him escape through the windows. It was at this juncture that policemen rushed in to restore order. While the law enforcement officers were busy disarming the combatants and leading them out, my eyes caught something moving underneath the seats. There, lo and behold, was the Minister of Finance crawling out from his hiding place. He had successfully missed active service!

With Parliament evacuated by policemen, I hurried back to the office. Everyone was in a state of excitement. All the offices and departments were empty. People had trooped out to watch the drama and when it all ended, everyone was too excited to settle down to work. Very soon, the whole Secretariat was empty, no one bothered to wait until office closing hours.

Next morning, the drama continued. Only this time the scene of conflict had changed from the Parliament buildings to the Premier's office. The two Premiers were still at large, each one surrounded by his followers. When I arrived office, the Permanent Secretary summoned us to a meeting, to instruct us on how to go about our work in the present circumstances. He informed us that Prime Minister Ladele had telephoned him that morning, to say he would soon be coming to the office, and had requested for certain papers to be ready for him by the time he arrived. Our Permanent Secretary explained to us that we were civil servants and therefore, we were not expected to take sides. Our duty was to serve loyally, whichever government emerged. He reminded us of the ethics of the civil service, which is, that a civil servant must observe the triple maxim of impartiality, anonymity and neutrality. He expounded at length on the importance of political neutrality.

He was still warming up to his lecture when we heard the sound of trumpets. Apparently, Premier Ladele had got his followers to acquire some trumpets and blow them after him as a demonstration of authority and power. Our meeting broke up in confusion as the Permanent Secretary, who was also Secretary to the Premier, must be waiting outside to receive the incoming Premier. Once again, excitement kindled all over the Secretariat. People trooped out of their offices to watch the strange spectacle of a Premier arriving, accompanied by a fanfare of trumpets and drums. And wonders of all wonders, there were no less than twenty lorries loaded with people chanting war songs.

The Premier alighted from his car, was met by the Permanent

Secretary and led to his office accompanied by drummers, some went before him singing his praises and pouring abuses on his rival. No less than fifty thugs and muscle-men stood guard, carrying dangerous weapons and charms. They marched up and down along the corridors of the offices, with a menancing air about them. All the civil servants who trooped out to watch the spectacle had to smile to them or put up their fingers in victory sign, in order to avoid being beaten up.

On entering his office, Premier Ladele went and sat behind his desk, and started giving instructions to his Secretary. Some emergency laws had to be drafted immediately, an official report must be made to the Federal Government in Lagos, with an urgent request for more police protection. A curfew had to be imposed immediately. Some of us, officials, who had entered with our Permanent Secretary, stood inside the office and looked with pity at him, for he could hardly hear what the Premier was saying, nor could he make himself heard because of the noise of the drummers and the thugs who had forced their way inside. In vain the Premier tried to keep them silent. As far as they were concerned, it was a day of entertainment, and nothing would detract them from their fun and merry-making.

After about half an hour, Premier Ladele got up to go. He gave strict instructions that the doors to his office were to be locked and that, under no circumstances should anyone, other than himself, be allowed inside. As he came out of the building to enter his car, the noise of drumming and singing went into crescendo, while the numerous retinue scrambled into the twenty escort lorries, brandishing cudgels, matchets and other dangerous weapons.

We locked the Prime Minister's office and went to our different offices but no one could settle down to work. Little did we know that the day's excitement had just begun. Not quite an hour after the first Premier left with his retinue, the second Premier appeared. Once again, pandemonium rent the air. Hundreds of market women and youngsters chanting war songs appeared on the wide double lane leading to the Secretariat. They molested every vehicle passing by. Passengers were forced to get out of their vehicles and were thoroughly abused.

Premier Rotimi advanced slowly amidst the throng of disorderly crowd. When his car finally stopped in front of the office, it took another fifteen minutes before he could enter the building. Market

women danced and sang, one of the escort lorries suddenly discharged a load of masquerades who pranced about with all sorts of agile displays.

Now the officials in the Premier's office were at a loss as to what to do. The first Premier had issued strict instructions, that on no account, was his office to be opened to anyone, except himself. Now, here was a second Premier slowly but steadfastly advancing towards the door. Our Permanent Secretary sensing trouble, went out through the back door of his office and disappeared. We took our cue from him and each of us - Under Secretary, Senior Assistant Secretaries, Assistant Secretaries and all fled in different directions.

Premier Rotimi finally reached the door of his office and found it securely locked. He sent for the Permanent Secretary, but he was nowhere to be found. What about the Under Secretary? What about all the other officials? The response he got was the same - they were nowhere to be found.

Premier Rotimi stood bewildered in front of the door. He managed a smile, but everyone could see that he was in a state of embarrassment. He was not to wait for long. Three of his followers, political thugs came to his rescue. They approached and asked what was the problem. Without any hesitation, they moved backwards a few steps and then charged at the door. On the second attempt, the door flew into pieces, blown off completely. Premier Rotimi made a triumphant entry amidst his unruly followers chanting war songs.

He seated himself at the Premier's desk and his followers gave a great shout of victory. One of them suggested that a photographer should be summoned to take the photograph of Premier Rotimi, seated at his desk and transacting his official duties. This suggestion was hailed as a brilliant one for, after all, photographs do not lie.

FOURTEEN

After three or four days of disappearance, our Permanent Secretary eventually emerged from his hide-out. By then, it had become inevitable, that there would be fresh elections to choose a proper government, after the fracas on the floor of the Legislature. It was obvious that the elections would be fiercely contested and that no holds would be barred.

One political party chose the cock as its symbol. The rival party promptly took the opportunity to slaughter a cock at every political campaign rally. When the cock had been killed, its head would be buried in full view of the spectators and the decapitated dead cock will be held up to signify victory over the rival party. Of course, the party with the cock were not slow to retaliate; their opponents had chosen a symbol which they said symbolised abundant wealth, children and plentiful harvest for all. This symbol was the banana tree, noted for its rapid multiplication. At every political rally, the party of the cock included in their entourage a lorry load of monkeys devouring bananas and messing up the lorry and everywhere. The lorry would be paraded round the spectators, while the party stalwarts drew attention to the fate awaiting bananas.

As the day of the elections drew near, the excitement and anxieties rose to fever point. Back home in my village, the Head Chief rose at dawn and holding a juju in his hand, he went round the village to put a curse on anyone who would vote for the Cock Party. The Cock Party reacted by threatening him that if their Party won the elections he would be deposed and deported to a forbidden bush where he would spend the rest of his life.

River Owena flowed and meandered through some part of the States. On the left of the river were people who supported the Banana party, while on the right of the river the population favoured the Cock Party. Boundary disputes had been the main cause of their disagreement. As the elections drew near, the Banana Party, which was far richer than its rival, bribed the electoral officers to erect most of the polling booths for the election on the left side of the river. They then approached the owners of the canoes plying the river, bought up all the canoes for the election day. When the day came, the inhabitants on the right side of the

65

river woke up to find that they had no means of reaching the polling booths on the other side of the river to cast their votes. In the meantime, party faithfuls on the other side danced up and down the river-side, daring their opponents to swim or fly across the river.

I came back from work one afternoon to find my cousin from home waiting for me. He was a good-for-nothing fellow, who did not believe in hard work, but looked for easy ways to make a living. Naturally, he came to me almost every month to sponge on me and touch me for a few Naira. I should have resented him and told him never to visit me, but he had his own good qualities which endeared him to me. He was always ready to attend to my mother and run errands for her. In the burning heat of the sun or in blinding rain, he trekked up and down the streets or sometimes journeying to the neighbouring villages on my mother's service. And so my heart always melted whenever I saw him, and I shed off a few Naira which I could hardly afford.

But wonder of all wonders! I came back from work to find him with a bulky suit-case filled to the brim - shoes, shirts and all sorts of wearing apparels. He greeted me with a mischievous grin on his face. When I asked him to explain how he came by the sudden wealth, he asked me to help him pray that there would always be elections every year. He had been recruited by the Banana Party to carry ballot boxes loaded with ballot papers to polling stations secretly on polling day. In addition he had been provided with acid to pour into the ballot boxes of political opponents. The Party have paid him handsomely, with a promise of more money when the assignment was completed.

I reminded him of the risk he was taking. If he was caught, he would be jailed. He merely laughed heartily and reminded me that everything in this world was a risk, and cited the example of the food that people put into their mouths; it could go into the wrong pipe and then you choke and die. He even reminded me that a taxi could knock me down on the way from work and kill me.

I had meant to give him a pep talk on the risks of his new occupation, but to my greatest chagrin it was he who started to lecture me. "Look, Brother," he said, "all these books you have been reading all your life, was it not because you want money? How much do they pay you in a whole year? Look at me now, I never went to any college but today I can employ a graduate to carry those ballot boxes after me and I will pay him better than what government pays you people."

I listened to him, half in anger and half in amusement. I summoned all the patience I could to remind him again of the risk of imprisonment. "Brother," he crowed joyously , " you only know books, you don't know what is going on in the world. You see, , there is nothing like a political party. Last week, the police rounded us up for two days; on the third day, the police opened our cell and told us to go away. We went straight to the house of the party leader where we were feted and given plenty of money.

Amidst violence and rigging of elections, the results of the election were announced. The Cock party had lost in the elections, but they believed that the other party had achieved victory by tricks and fraud. This was when violence took over. The Cock party and their followers took to the streets, burning houses and motor vehicles. When this was not sufficient to assuage their anger they resorted to burning their opponents alive. This they achieved by the simple process of pouring petrol on their victims and setting them alight.

I travelled home for the week-end. I called on a friend who was a lecturer at one of our universities and who had been in the front-line of the Banana party. He was not at home but I saw his mother. As his mother set her eyes on me she ran to meet me and shouted, "Praise God! praise God for me that your friend did not bring sorrow on me in my old age." So saying, she burst into tears. I was bewildered. What was she trying to tell me? Had my friend been involved in a motor accident? I tried to calm her down to tell me what happened but she had collapsed in tears.

Later, I got the story of what happened to my friend, when his brother walked in. The local members of the Cock Party had started on a rampage, burning the houses and motor vehicles of their political opponents. That morning they had already roasted two of their opponents alive. Then they advanced towards the house of my friend, the lecturer who was like a rat trapped in a hole, they surrounded the house and got ready to set fire to it. Sensing the imminent danger, he attempted to escape through the back door. Unfortunately for him, he landed in the hands of his enemies. They held him, opened the jerry-can of petrol and poured it on him, ready to set him ablaze. The leader of the gang dipped his hands into his pocket to bring out the box of matches and then discovered that there were no matches left. None of his followers had any matches on them. Still holding the lecturer, he then sent one of them to the nearest store to buy matches. At an unguarded moment, my friend tore off his clothes, shook himself free and fled half naked, while his enemies pursued him down the street. He sighted a friend's car, jumped inside and with all the petrol dripping down into the car he escaped to safety.

FIFTEEN

The controversial elections had come and gone. The leader of the Banana party came to power and was appointed Premier. On his first day in the office he summoned all the senior officials for a briefing. Our Permanent Secretary got up and made a welcome speech, congratulating the new Premier on his victory at the elections and pledging the support and loyalty of all the civil servants to him and his administration.

The Permanent Secretary had hardly resumed his seat when we heard a commotion at the door. It appeared that someone was trying to force his way into the Premier's office. The Permanent Secretary asked me to go and find out what was happening. It was one of the Premier's party men. The Premier ordered that he should be allowed to come in. The man, walking with a walking-stick, burst into the room and walked with long strides, fury written all over his face. The Premier was the first to greet him. "Good Afternoon, Chief Folami, I hope there is nothing wrong?"

Chief Folami, pointing his walking-stick at the Premier, bellowed out "You hope there is nothing wrong? You will soon know that something is wrong, you this liar, you unreliable man. I will show you. I will use every energy and power that God gave me to ruin you and your party. If you last the next six months as Premier, then I am not Chief Folami . . ."

The Prime Minister was surprisingly calm. "Now, Chief Folami, calm down, what is it all about? What can be so serious that we cannot sit down calmly and resolve it? Sit down; Permanent Secretary, please offer Chief Folami a chair."

Once again, the walking-stick went up pointing straight at the Premier's face. "Didn't you promise me that if the Party won the elections, you would appoint me as a Minister? I have listened on the radio to the list of names of your new Ministers and my name is not amongst them. You are a liar; no one can rely on you. But this time, you will regret the day you lied to me. I will finish you. From today, I will devote all my time and energy to ensure that I ruin you and your Party."

With this, Chief Folami landed his walking-stick on the Premier's table with such violence that everything on it rattled and the Premier was visibly shaken. Chief Folami stormed out and slammed the door with a loud bang.

The Premier shouted after him, "Chief Folami, come back, listen to me." In panic, the Premier asked one of the officials sitting in front of him to run out and bring Chief Folami back. He returned to the room with a look of contempt and defiance on his face. The Premier offered him a seat, and then turned to the Permanent Secretary. He said, "Permanent Secretary, a little while ago when you were briefing me about the various Ministries, I remember that you mentioned Ministry of Health and Social Welfare. Am I correct?" Our Permanent Secretary confirmed that the Premier was right. Then the Premier's face lighted up with joy and the eyes were twinkling with mischief and triumph. He continued, "why do you civil servants like to tie together things which should be left separately alone? You like to tie a goat with a ram and a turkey with a chicken. Why do you tie Health with Social Welfare?"

The Premier then turned to Chief Folami who had listened to the dialogue between the Premier and his Permanent Secretary with a puzzled look. "Chief Folami," announced the Premier; "From this moment, I appoint you as Minister of Social Welfare. Permanent Secretary, prepare the necessary announcements and arrange to separate those things." Chief Folami jumped up from his seat and roared with laughter. He ran to the Premier and hugged him. Then he turned to the officials and shook our hands one by one, saying, "Ah, Yes, this is how things ought to be among friends. The Premier is a great man and a great leader. That is why we all love and respect him. I am prepared to follow him through thick and thin." And with this, he danced out of the room.

Now there was a look of consternation and distress on the face of our Permanent Secretary. He turned to the Premier and with a nervous cough he said "Your Excellency, please permit me to make one or two observations. I am making them out of my loyalty to you and my anxiety to see that you and your new administration succeed. In the first place, there is no rationale or sense of logic in breaking one Ministry into two, especially during this period of financial austerity. I was still going to brief you on our precarious financial situation. In the second place, your Excellency, I know Chief Folami intimately well. He is hardly literate. He cannot comprehend the memos and papers that will come before him as a Minister." The Premier could hardly contain his anger. He exploded, "what have all these things you are talking got to do with the problem on nand? You know nothing about politics; confine yourself to your civil service. Whether or not Chief Folami can read or write is completely irrelevant and immaterial."

And with this, the Premier and his new administration assumed the reins of power.

SIXTEEN

For some time now, there had been rumours in the air that a promotion exercise was going on and all of us who were involved became nervous. One of our colleagues had close family connection with the Head of Civil Service. We often met in his office to know if he had any information. He would put on a knowing look, hint very vaguely that the outcome was going to be a shock to quite a number of us but we got nothing concrete from him. In due course, we discovered that he was nowhere near the source of information and we stopped assembling in his office.

Then a brilliant idea occurred to us. The Confidential Secretary to a boss was the keeper of all his secrets. She often sat at meetings to take notes and she typed confidential matters for the boss. Why not cultivate the friendship of the Confidential Secretary to the Head of Civil Service? But then who will bell the cat? Here was a formidable lady whose dressing and appearance, not to mention her gait and style of walking, proclaimed a high class lady, who would never hob-nob with small fries like ourselves. However, one of us who had always been a play-boy disagreed with this assessment. He held a contrary view. In a tone of authority, he assured us that those were the class of ladies who were easiest to conquer. His reason was that they were not after money, but they were often hungry for something else - sex. "Get her into bed, occupy her from night till morning without stopping and she becomes your slave for ever," he asserted with authority. We all hailed him and asked if he would undertake the assignment. For a brief moment his face fell, but he quickly realised that he had led us on too far to back out. He squared his shoulders and volunteered to conquer the high and mighty Secretary to the Head of Civil Service. One snag, though, he pointed out, this type of assignment required Dutch courage. He needed to be fortified with plenty of drinks to bolster up his courage as he set out to meet her. Would we be willing to make some contribution towards the cost of his beer and occasional whisky?

We waited for four weeks and our colleague was not able to produce any result, indeed he had not as much as ventured near the lady's residence. In those four weeks each of us had parted with our pocket money to pay for his drinks. We decided to try

another channel. This time we would use the boss's messenger. Messengers are known to have free access to the office of their boss, entering at will to take out files and bring in files and other papers. We sent for the messenger in the office of the Head of Civil Service and promised to ensure his speedy promotion. We told him what to do. One of us, who was working in that office was asked to receive and read the file when the messenger brought it out.

Again, to our greatest chagrin, another four weeks passed when the messenger brought out every imaginable file but not the relevant one. Our Head of Civil Service was no doubt a man of experience and knew what havoc messengers and other junior officials in the office could perpetrate. Indeed, we soon discovered that even, his Confidential Secretary was not let into the secrets of the promotion exercise. We gave up the hunt and whistled around "whatever will be, will be."

SEVENTEEN

Then one fine morning, I reached the office and found an official brown envelope addressed to me. The envelope bore the stamp of the office of the Head of Civil Service. I looked at it and circled the table three times before picking it up. Since I had not committed any offence, nor been on trial for any offence, I guessed that whatever was inside the envelope must be good news - long-awaited good news. I picked the envelope up and danced round the room. Finally, burning with excitement and joy, I tore open the envelope. Then my face fell. What was this? I had been chosen to participate at a seminar taking place in Lagos the following week. I was to prepare and submit a report on my return. I sat down heavily on my chair and anger welled up within me. The expected promotion had not come and now I was to labour on the submission of a report; another factor that would determine my suitability or otherwise for promotion.

I was in bad spirits for the rest of the day, snapping at everybody. My luckless typist and messenger took the brunt of my foul temper. "Can't you see that I am busy? Do you have to slam the door so loud? Can't you speak up or am I expected to apply ears to your mouth? Where have you been? I have been buzzing you for the past half hour. Gone to eat? Without the courtesy of telling me? What is the service coming to these days?"

We were near to closing time when the Permanent Secretary sent for me. There was to be a Conference of the National Economic Council in Lagos and I was to be on the Premier's entourage to act as Secretary. I would be in charge of all support arrangements - accommodation, transport, supervising the typists, ensuring that papers and memorandum were prepared and delivered to all on time and acting as general liaison officer.

Of course, I was not intimidated by this assignment. I had undertaken a similar assignment when I was in the Ministry of Health. Indeed, I had been praying for another opportunity to spend two or three days in a posh hotel in Lagos. Free food, free drinks, wonderful sleep in an air-conditioned room, a luxurious bath, such as I never saw in my rented room, where there was a common cubicle at the back of the house for all the occupants of the house. You either rushed out to the back of the house long

"WHERE WAS THIS YOUR BOGUS REPORT WHEN THIS MATTER WAS TABLED THREE DAYS AGO."

before day-break to have your bath or you waited on a long queue later in the morning while you cursed and kicked your feet. But now for three glorious days, I was to live in luxury.

The first day passed off peacefully at the Conference. The President was in the chair and the conference sat state by state, each state led by its Premier and Deputy Premier. On the second day, however, there was a memorandum which sparked off trouble. It was the siting of the Iron and Steel industry in the country. Each state recognized its technological importance and the advantages that would accrue if the industry was sited in a particular state. And so every state went all out to get the conference to agree to site the industry in its state.

There was the Eastern State which was smarter than the rest. It had got a team of experts from Europe to produce a report which showed that the East possessed all the ingredients and offered the best advantages for the industry. The Premier asked for permission to distribute the report to members. Immediately, our Premier saw that the East had pulled a fast one over everybody. At this juncture, our Premier prayed the President to suspend debate on the matter to enable members to study the various papers distributed at the Conference. Everyone agreed.

Immediately the Conference adjourned for the day, the Premier summoned us all to his residence, asked the Permanent Secretary for Economic Development to fly out that very night and look for experts to write a report that would show that our State was the most suitable place for the siting of the Iron and Steel industry. As time was against us, all that happened was that we got some back-wood firm of consultants to adopt the report which we had ourselves prepared and to put their name on it. It was beautifully typed and bound with a glossy cover.

The Permanent Secretary flew in on the last evening of the Conference. Next morning, debates opened on the siting of the Iron and Steel Industry. The East reminded the Conference of the Report of experts which showed that the East was endowed with all the infra-structure than any other State in the country. Our Premier jumped up and brandished his own Report which proved conclusively that, nowhere else in the whole Federation was better suited for the siting of the industry than his own State.

The Eastern Premier flew into a rage. "Where was your bogus report when this matter was tabled three days ago?" he asked. Our

Premier was instantly on his feet. "Mr. President, ask him to withdraw the word "bogus", or else trouble will erupt in this hall today. How dare you describe my report as bogus? It is far more authentic and more authoritative than the rubbish which some crooks wrote for you."

Now several people rose to their feet, brandishing their fists and shouting at one another across the room. Two or three Commissioners brought out their walking-sticks and threatened to use them on the heads of their opponents. There was utter pandemonium. Amidst all the din, the President sat calm and unruffled, looking from one side to the other. He kept banging the gavel in front of him on the table and shouting, "Gentlemen, Gentlemen, Order, Order." No one listened to him, as indeed, no one heard.

This state of anarchy went on for about fifteen minutes when the President managed to restore order. Then our Deputy Premier was on his feet, claiming the attention of the House. He was a bearded burly-looking man, wide chested who looked more suited for pugilistic career than for sitting at conference tables. He was now thoroughly on the war path, determined to avenge the affront on his Premier by the other State Premiers. He started on an inflammatory speech which was promptly cut short by the opponent Premier who jumped up from his seat and shouted, "Mr. President, call that yokel to order; I am not his rank; a running water seeks its own level; let him find his level." Our Deputy Premier was about to unleash all the fury inside him, when our Premier got up and said, "Mr. President, my colleague from the East has claimed a higher rank than my deputy; but ask him, Mr. President, has he got a beard like that of my deputy, has he got the chest like that of my deputy?"

With this, the whole Conference dissolved into laughter and while the laughter still lasted, the President hastily adjourned the Conference and members trooped out, some laughing and some threatening trouble at the next Conference.

EIGHTEEN

It was mid-morning. The door opened and my messenger dropped a letter on my desk. I glanced at it casually and noticed that it was an official envelope. I dismissed it from my mind as one of those tedious circulars on seminars and economic measure. Not quite long after, one of my colleagues in the Ministry of Education burst in. He was ecstatic with joy and excitement. I looked at him and wondered the cause of his jubilation. "Did you not receive your own letter?" he asked me. "What letter?" I countered back. "What letter, promotion of course." "Promotion!" I exclaimed. Then my attention settled on the letter which was dropped on my desk a little while ago. I tore it open hurriedly and there I read,

"Dear Mr. Alade,

I am pleased to inform you that the Civil Service Commission has approved your promotion to the rank of Senior Assistant Secretary with effect from 1st July.
Please accept my congratulations.

Signed
Head of Civil Service."

I sprang up from my chair and hugged my colleague. We both shouted and hailed each other. We started telephoning our other colleagues to ask if they too had received the happy news. That evening, we congregated at our usual haunt to celebrate. Empty bottles of beer littered the ground while those yet to be opened glistened with condensation. In the morning, I dressed specially for the office, wearing my Sunday suit which our local people call, 'bottom box.' On arriving at the office, all the junior officers in the Department came rushing in to congratulate me. I could see a look of greater respect in their eyes and in the form of their greetings. Even the Confidential Secretary to the Permanent Secretary dropped in to offer her congratulations and I could sense by the way she held my hand that she now considered me an eligible suitor.

With my new status, I knew that I could not stay longer on my present assignment and therefore, it was no surprise when a few days later, a Circular letter titled 'Postings' came out and I found my name on the list, posted to the Ministry of Local Government. Here was the domain of the Deputy Governor, where he presided over the Ministry as if it was a separate kingdom. With his profuse beard and blood-shot eyes, his appearance was indeed intimidating.

After meeting my Permanent Secretary, I went to the Deputy Premier to pay my respects. On seeing me his eyes lit up and he enthused all over me. "Ah, that is Alade, I have seen a lot of you in the Premier's office and I am told you are one of our very bright men. Excellent, excellent, just what I need right now. Sit down, Alade; you see, in this Ministry, we have now moved to the stage of Operation Total." He paused to answer a telephone call while I was lost in puzzle as to what he meant.

Putting down the telephone, he resumed his talk. "You see, elections will be held next year. I am determined to break the back of our political opponents and wipe off all opposition from this state. It is you that I will be using most of the time; your Permanent Secretary is always busy attending all sorts of useless meetings in the office of the Head of Civil Service. I hardly ever see him when I need him. Now, Alade, the war has commenced and let me give you your first assignment right away. I want all local government councils controlled by the opposition party to be dissolved; I think they are about 39 in all. They must all be dissolved, no exception. Now go and start working on that and submit your proposals to me by the end of the week."

I rose and left his office in bewilderment. On reaching my office, I called for the records and files of all the local government councils controlled by the opposition party. After three days of hard reading, except for one or two councils I could find no serious faults with any of the councils to warrant dissolution. I therefore made a submission to the Deputy Premier, pointing out that there was no justification in dissolving any of the local government councils which he has in mind.

Next day, the Deputy Premier sent for me. As I entered his office he looked up and said, "Morning, Mr. Alade, are you sure that this Ministry is going to accommodate both of us." "Beg your pardon, Sir," I stammered. "I don't understand your meaning Sir." "Look, Alade, what else can I say when you put on the garb of a saint and you make me look like the devil incarnate?" My puzzle and confusion became deeper.

"A few days ago, I gave you clear instructions to prepare necessary papers to dissolve 39 local government councils. Now, what do

I get back in reply? Get one thing straight from today henceforth, Mr. Alade, If I were a priest and preaching from the pulpit, I would reason exactly the way you had done. If I were in a court of law with my wig on my head, I would reason like you have done. But when I am sitting in this chair, I am not a priest, nor a judge of the High Court. I am not a reasonable human being. I am a politician and my sole aim is power and victory over my political opponents, no matter the means or the method. Now take your file back and find those local government councils guilty of one serious offence or the other. Prepare the Order for their dissolution. Later in the day, I will give you the names of my party men who will constitute management committees in place of those bastards."

I left the Deputy Premier's office feeling dazed as though I had just woken up from a bad dream. By the time I reached my office, there was a group of men in flowing robes waiting for me and talking noisily. You could see every sign of arrogance and defiance on their faces. I asked them politely, "What can I do for you, Gentlemen?" The one who looked like their leader said, "we have been waiting for you; has the Deputy Premier signed the order to dissolve those Councils? That is the file you are holding, is it not? We must take the news with us back home. Those idiots must begin to feel pepper in their eyes as from today. Have you sent the announcement to the radio?"

"Gentlemen," I answered with as much self-control as I could muster, "I do not work for you; if you want any information, why not go and see the Deputy Premier himself."

They left my office fuming with anger. I could distinctly hear them pour all sorts of abuses and invectives on me. One of them swore that I belong to the opposite political party and they must warn the Deputy Premier that an enemy had been planted in the Ministry who will frustrate and sabotage government plans. I went home that day feeling very depressed.

Next morning was not without its own surprises. I had hardly settled down in my office when my messenger came in to announce that there were about twelve people waiting to see me urgently. They were ushered in. Since there were only two chairs in my office, they had to stand. The leader of the delegation introduced himself and his men. They belonged to the opposition party in the State.

"Mr. Alade" the leader began. "You may not know us individually but we know you very well when you were in the Premier's office. Your reputation for impartiality and honesty is well known throughout the State. By God's Grace very soon you will be Permanent Secretary and one day you will become our Head of Civil Service. People like you who cannot be bought or threatened deserve to rise to the highest position in our country."

By this time, I was getting impatient, I had a very busy and crowded day before me. It was easy for me to see that all the man had said was all flattery and that he was on to something. But what was it? I tried to show my impatience by picking up one or two files on my desk and pretending to check on something. I think he got the message.

"Mr. Alade," he resumed. "We have reliable information that you have been asked to prepare papers for the dissolution of all the local government councils belonging to our party. We know that you are a God-fearing man and that you will not lend yourself to do the Deputy Premier's evil work for him. Let him do his own dirty work for himself; we know where to catch him and he will regret it for the rest of his life."

At last, I ventured to put in a word. "Gentlemen, I am not allowed to speak about what goes on in the office. Go and see my Minister". At this, they all stormed out threatening me with hell and fire. One remarked, "he has been bought; from today we must declare him an enemy and deal with him when the time comes."

In due course, the Deputy Premier who was my Commissioner took a curious liking for me and even nicknamed me "the Artful Dodger," after one of Charles Dickens's famous characters. The fact was that I had devised various subtle means of stalling, or playing for time or side-tracking orders and directives which I considered unreasonable or not in the public interest. Quite often, I would approach him when I knew that he was in a receptive mood. At such times he was prepared to see the daily political battle as a game to be enjoyed, with concessions made here and there. He was disposed to talk freely with me because I had since been promoted Deputy Permanent Secretary.

"Alade, I see with you" he would say, laughing unproariously while his beard bubbled back and forth. "I just wanted to scare them a bit and get them running around in panic." Perhaps he was in this frame of mind when he called me one morning and told me that he had decided to depose one of the great paramount traditional rulers in the State. I opened my mouth in alarm and disbelief. This will surely rock the State to the bottom.

Without waiting for me to speak, he opened his brief-case and drew out some papers. "I believe we have to make it look proper and legal, so we will conduct a Tribunal of Enquiry," the Deputy Premier told me. "Here are the Terms of Reference; he would be found guilty on every count, and here on this other sheet are the findings of the Tribunal."

At last, I could no longer contain myself. I said, "Did you say "findings", Deputy Premier? On an enquiry not yet conducted? Suppose the Tribunal finds him innocent of the charges preferred against him?" The Deputy Premier was completely unperturbed. He said, "Alade, I don't like that look on your face; you look as if you have seen the devil himself. I know you always like to sound holy, but I have warned you before that we are not here to conduct a Church revival service. This is politics; it is a form of war and all is fair in love and war. That paramount ruler has been working secretly against the interest of our party and the time has come to give it back to him. After he has been deposed, we shall banish him to some God-forsaken corner of the country."

NINETEEN

Rumours were getting stronger each day that one of us was to be posted to the Western Nigeria office in London. The mere thought of the choice falling on me filled me with such delight that I became dizzy with day-dreaming. I had never left the shores of Nigeria. I had all my education in Nigeria. I had read stories about life in England and America. They sounded like fairy-land tales and I had often wondered if luck or destiny would take me to those fairy-lands.

Already, it was rumoured that two of my colleagues had started lobbying to be selected for the posting. They were said to be using their family connections with the Head of the Civil Service, while the father of the other one was married to a close relation of the wife of the Head of Civil Service. These rumours filled me with fear and anxiety and entirely dampened my spirits.

Then came one of the happiest days of my life. I had just settled down in my office for the day, when I got a telephone message that the Head of Civil Service wanted to see me at 11 o'clock. My heart missed a beat. The great boss had never sent for me since I joined the Civil Service. Had I done something wrong which had been reported to him? Could it be in connection with the London posting that I had been day-dreaming about? My temperature immediately started to rise. Already I could feel some rumblings in my stomach. I jumped up and headed for the toilet.

I looked at the time; I had nearly two hours to go before my appointment. I examined my clothes. I was not particularly at my best. I dashed out and went home to change into a smarter suit. Minutes before the appointed time, I was in the office of the Secretary to the Head of Service. I sat down and picked up one of the periodicals on the centre-table. I flicked through the pages without seeing a single word. My ears and eyes were trained on the door leading to the office of the Head of Service and on the telephone on top of the Secretary's desk.

Shortly after, the door of the office opened, and there was the Head of Civil Service seeing off two gentlemen. He shook their hands at the door and then he saw me. "Mr. Alade, is it?" "Yes, Sir, Good Morning, Sir," I managed to croak, my throat suddenly becoming constricted

"Come right in, Alade," beamed the big boss, opening the door wider and ushering me inside his office. I followed him feeling like a lamb being led for the slaughter.

"Alade, how are you getting on these days?" he began. I managed a smile and said that I was getting on well. "Let me come straight to the point. How would you like to have a spell of time at our London office?" I could hardly believe my ears, to hear my dreams coming true. My heart was beating fast and I prayed that I may not say a wrong thing that would make him change his mind. "I would be very glad to go, Sir," I replied. "Good; I see you were married recently; how would your wife take the news?" "I am sure she would like it too, Sir," I replied. He persisted: "you better discuss it with her first; you are new in the world of married life and one of the things you will discover is that women can be very unpredictable." Now, I was growing anxious not to leave the matter in the air and undecided before I left his presence. Now, that I see my dreams coming true, I was not going to take any chances, especially when I knew that there were other people lobbying for the posting. I made another determined effort: "I am sure, Sir, that my wife would be most delighted. She had been looking forward for an opportunity for us to travel abroad." "Very well, Alade, I wish we could all be so sure about our wives. How soon can you be ready to fly? Suppose we say in three weeks time? Your posting to London will be for three years in the first instance. I will advise that you fly out quickly and when you are quite settled, your wife can join you."

Now, there are moments of great joy in one's life, when it is so over-whelming that one is at a loss as to how to give vent to one's feelings. This was one such moment for me. As I left the Head of Civil Service and the door closed behind me, I felt like dancing, I felt like whistling, I felt like shouting to the whole world that I was the happiest of men. Instead of returning to my office, I drove straight to the school where my wife was teaching. She was surprised to see me and from the look on my face, she could tell immediately that I had very good news for her. When I told her the news, she gave such a shout of joy, that it attracted the headmaster and other teachers. Although we felt slightly embarrassed, we hugged each other and sealed it all with a sweet kiss.

Three weeks later, I was in the plane bound for London. It was my first flight. From childhood, I had looked up at the sky when an aeroplane was passing by and I had always wondered how it was possible for human beings to be inside a machine so high up. Much as I wanted to experience air-travel, I dreaded the thought of being suspended in the firmament. My fear had always been further heightened by the news of aeroplane crashes that one reads about now and again.

But now, I had no option. I was inside the plane. On the announcement of, "Fasten your seat belt," my temperature started to rise. No sooner had the plane risen from the ground than another announcement came on. It was the captain, informing passengers that we were flying at an altitude of 36,000 feet. I did a mental calculation in miles, and this came to about seven miles. To imagine that I was hanging in the air seven miles from the ground! A cold sweat broke out from the back of my neck and trickled down my spine. I looked round at the faces of other passengers to see if they were passing through the same ordeal with me. I noticed that one or two closed their eyes tight, while another gripped the arms of his seat. Now my fear almost became a panic. I started to recite all the Psalms I could remember:

The Lord is my Shepherd, I shall not want;
He maketh me to lie down in green pastures...

But I was not now lying in green pastures. I was seven miles suspended in the firmament.

Yea, though I walked through the valley of the
shadow of death, I will fear no evil, for thou
art with me

But this was not a case of walking through the valley of death. I wish it was. Then I would have run fast to get out of it. I was seven miles hanging in a machine in the sky and I could neither walk nor run from the danger.

Not quite long after, a stewardess was passing by laden with assorted drinks. It suddenly occured to me that this might be an answer to my problems. Even though I had hardly ever drank liquor in all my life, I ordered a tall whisky. I repeated the order three times. I wanted to get drunk and lose consciousness, so that I would not be aware of whatever befell the plane. But I was soon to discover that there are certain emotional stresses which a state of drunkenness cannot overcome. Though I became drunk, I was still conscious of a sense of danger and each time the loud- speaker rumbled for an announcement, I would jump in my seat.

"Ladies and Gentlemen, we are now flying over the Mediterranean." A short while later, "Ladies and Gentlemen, we are flying over Spain and if you look to your left, you will see the city of Barcelona." But each time the loud-speaker rumbled, my heart jumped into my mouth, and I thought the end had come. I was pressed to attend the calls of nature, but I felt too scared to leave my seat. When it at last became unbearable, I staggered towards the toilet. I entered it and locked the door. The tiny cubicle shook and rattled and terrible fear gripped me. For a brief moment, the drinks cleared from my head and I began to recite Psalm 121:

"I will lift up my eyes to the hills.

From whence cometh my help?"...

But I could not even see any hill now. And even if I could, I would have to look down to see the hills, instead of lifting up my eyes as the Psalmist recommended.

I quickly got out of the toilet and staggered back to my seat. I remained in this state of fear and stupor until we landed.

As I stepped out of the plane, I felt a sense of great excitement. It was my first travel outside Nigeria. I had read a lot about England and often dreamt of visits to London. Here was I at last in the city of my dreams.

An official from the office came to meet me and took me to a little bed-and breakfast accommodation, which would be my residence until I am able to find a suitable flat. He came in the following morning to take me to the office. We left the apartment and started to walk. Three minutes later, we left the pavement and entered a building. My companion went on the queue to obtain a ticket. I started to wonder. Aren't we in London? Railway ticket to where again?

I followed him like a dog being led by the owner. Then wonder of all wonders! We started to descend steps into the ground! Presently we found ourselves on a railway platform. While I was still gaping with wonder a train roared into the station. I followed my guide inside. Even though it was crowded, no one took notice of each other. It was all silent. Some hid their faces behind their newspapers, while the majority merely stared into space oblivious of fellow passengers. How strange it all was to me, when I reflected on the general conviviality back at home in lorries where passengers coming together for the first time share jokes, exchange experiences and narrate incidents. I looked from face to face. It was all grim and cold.

Shortly after, we climbed up into the street and into the normal world of human beings. As we walked to our office, I noticed that everyone walking on the pavement seemed to be in a hurry. No one stopped to greet anyone. No one took notice of anyone. I wondered what sort of country England was! Presently, we entered the Nigeria High Commission Office and I was taken straight to the Head of the Office.

When I was ushered into his presence, the first thing that struck me about him was his elaborate and immaculate dress. He wore a three- piece suit of striped worsted woolen, a blue striped shirt of very expensive material and a silk tie to match. The breast pocket was adorned with a huge handkerchief. Two of his fingers shone with rings which he appeared to display ostentatiously at every gesture.

My immediate reaction was that I felt rather shabby and totally inferior. I was dressed in a suit sewn by local tailors in Nigeria; a suit which had seen better days but was still one of my favourites. It was altogether inappropriate for my new surroundings. I made a mental note to order suits, London tailored, as soon as the first salary comes in. I then shifted my attention from the man's clothes and concentrated on what he had to say to me. It was to be my first briefing in my new assignment.

It was the man's manner of speaking that amazed me. He had developed an accent and demeanour calculated to impress his listeners, no doubt, but which made him appear ridiculous. He seemed to be at pains to prove that he had imbibed English culture and manners, and that he had risen far above the ordinary African. As he spoke, he puffed up in his chair and kept using his left hand to brush his hair back, which unfortunately, there was little left of the hair, just a few tufts of dirty grey. There was no doubt that he was forever at great pains to impress people with his self-importance.

I listened to him as he spoke, expounding at length, while sometimes inspecting his glistening rings, no doubt to draw my attention to their beauty or value. On my part, being my first day in London, I was much too excited by everything around me, to listen to my boss who was apparently enjoying the sound of his own voice. At long last, he summoned an official to show me to my office. This was another glorious moment in my life. To imagine that I occupied an office, all to myself, in London. And what is more, a young West Indian lady soon appeared, all smiles and oozing charm. She introduced herself as my Secretary.

My Secretary! All to myself! Back at home, my grade was not entitled to a Secretary. I had shared a Secretary-Typist with another colleague. And here, standing before me and fussing on me was a lady of pink colour, with black hair flowing down to the shoulders and sparkling white teeth which glistened as she turned all her charms on me. She wore a simple, straight dress tied at the waist and cut square across the shoulders. Her mouth was small and full-lipped. It dominated her face which was set in a series of curves consisting of high cheek-bones, large slanted eyes and a cleft chin. A long and slender neck held up a small head which ended in one inward curve to her shoulders. She was my Secretary all to myself. I went into raptures of delight and mentally conjured up happy hours of blissful time with this delectable fair creature.

Unfortunately, my hopes with my beautiful secretary were soon to be shattered. I spent the first month sizing her up reconnoitering, looking for an opening and then alas, I lost her. The High Commissioner's Secretary had resigned and he had specifically asked for my Secretary to be posted to work with him. I cursed silently under my breath and for a long time I bore a grudge against the High Commissioner who stole my beautiful Secretary. The grudge became even deeper when another Secretary was posted to me whose very sight dampened my spirit and continually dulled my appetite. I kept her at arms length and ensured that I saw very little of her.

There was to be a meeting with the British Foreign and Commonwealth office. They wrote to suggest a date which was not convenient for me. I therefore wrote back:

"I am directed to refer to your letter in connection with the proposed meeting on employment of British nationals in Nigeria and to say that the date you proposed is not convenient. I am to ask that you let us know which date you prefer."

Three days later, my telephone rang. It was from a Mr. Baker and he referred to my letter. He asked if I could possibly be directed to fix a meeting for Wednesday the following week. I told him that I did not have to be directed and that I could give him the answer straight-away which was that Wednesday would be fine by me. He thanked me and then asked why I gave the impression that I was being directed in my earlier letter. I told him that this was our official mode of correspondence in Nigeria. Mr. Baker could not hide his surprise and amusement and he laughed at the other end of the line. I felt very stupid as I replaced the telephone.

We went to the Foreign and Commonwealth Office the following week. On getting to Mr. Baker's office he suggested that his big boss the Permanent Under-Secretary would be glad to say hello to us. The Permanent Under-Secretary was the equivalent of our Permanent Secretary in Nigeria. Mr. Baker took us to the next floor and along the corridor until we entered the office of his boss. To my greatest amazement, he opened the door and said, "Morning John, here are our friends from the Nigerian High Commission office." The big boss rose from his table, shook our hands and chatted with us for a few minutes. Then he said "let's see if the Minister is free; I am sure he will be delighted to see our Nigerian friends."

The Permanent Secretary himself led the way to the Minister's office; upon being told by the Minister's private secretary that the Minister was free, he opened the door, we walked in and he said to the Minister, "Bill, meet our friends from the Nigerian High Commission." The Minister was all smiles and exuding charm. I was stupefied with amazement! To imagine a relatively junior official calling his Permanent Secretary by his first name and again to hear the Permanent Secretary calling his Minister by his first name! What a world of difference from our Nigerian situation where everyone fiercely guarded his rank and would regard it as the greatest height of insult to be addressed by his first name by a junior person. If I returned to our office there in London and walked into the office of our boss and say, "Morning, James", he would give me a horrified look and wonder whether I was drunk or mad. Before the end of the day, he would certainly cable to Nigeria asking them to recall me home for gross impertinence.

"GET A LARGE CUP OR A JUG AND FILL IT WITH ORANGE JUICE THAT IS WHAT I NEED!"

TWENTY

London is a city of hotels and restaurants, great and small. Besides the exclusively residential areas, there is no street to which you turn and you will not find it dotted with hotels and places where you can pop in and get something to eat. Our office was situated on Great Portland Street, and right in the middle of the street was the Horse and Groom - a pub and restaurant combined. Officials from our office frequented this place and we were very familiar customers to the proprietors. But the proprietors could never hide their amusement each time they saw me appear at the door-way.

Whenever I came in for breakfast, I would ask for a glass of orange juice. The glass they produced was so tiny, hardly bigger than a little ink-pot, that I asked them to repeat the glass four times. Even after the fourth glass, I would beckon to the waiter and complain that the orange juice did not reach my stomach, it all disappeared somewhere between my mouth and my stomach, I was as dry as when I came in. Each time I said to the waiter, "Get a large cup or a jug and fill it with orange juice; that is what I need." The Manager and the waiter would exchange glances, hardly able to suppress their laughter. The same incident took place whenever I came in for lunch. This time, however, the quarrel would be about water. Unless you asked for water, the restaurant did not supply it. When you did, it came in a tiny little glass. This always made me lose my temper. I would summon the waiter and ask for a jug of water with a big glass to accompany it. This request, which came in a rather loud voice, always made the other guests in the restaurant, mainly white, to turn in my direction and look at me with amazement and curiousity.

I entered the restaurant one afternoon for lunch and to my greatest surprise, I saw an old school friend sitting quietly at a table. I had not seen him for over ten years. I remembered that he did not complete his secondary school education when he stowed away to England and had since lived a precarious existence, often on the outer fringes of the law.

We hugged each other, and oblivious of the presence of other guests in the restaurant, my friend kept shouting my school days nickname at the top of his voice. As usual, all the other guests turned to look in our direction and I felt greatly embarrassed. After all, I was a senior official of the Nigerian High Commission, attired in a three-piece suit with pocket handkerchief and tie to match. But my friend had no such inhibitions. His hair and beard were unkempt and his shirt and shoes looked like something dug out of a dustbin. But he was cheerful and seemed to have no cares at all in the world.

I sat with him and we started to reminisce, recalling all the past. He asked about the whereabout of several old colleagues. He asked what I was doing in London and I told him about my job in the Nigerian Embassy. At the mention of Nigerian Embassy, he became like a bull which has seen red cloth. He turned wild and poured abuses and curses on the Embassy and every official in the place. In his opinion, they were not there to assist any Nigerian; the officials were a bunch of arrogant and selfish idiots, earning money for doing no work. I tried in vain to persuade him of the usefulness of the office. I offered to take him to the office but he swore never to step his feet into the Nigeria High Commission office.

As his company was becoming irksome to me, I looked pointedly at my wrist-watch and got up. Outside on the street, he asked me how I spent my evenings and suggested that I needed to see some of the fun in London at night. I told him that I had been to some of the cinema houses to watch films and that they were very interesting. He laughed very loud and said that was not his idea of fun and that he must show me exciting places in London. We agreed to meet in front of the cinema in Leicester Square the following Monday at nine o'clock in the evening. And with this, we parted.

Monday evening came. I thought of what excuse to give to my wife for going out. Usually, we went out together in the evenings to watch films or visit friends. I set out, first on a bus and later changed to an underground train which brought me directly to Leicester Square. I emerged from the underground and waited in front of the cinema. One hour passed the time of our appointment and there was no sign of my good friend. It was going to eleven o'clock and I had decided to call it off and return home, when I saw him sauntering towards me. I could not hide my anger for keeping me waiting for so long. But he was completely unperturbed; his dress was even worse than on the previous occasion, consisting of a coarse and faded sweater on top of shabby corduroy trousers. I looked out of place in my well-cut suit. He had no apologies for being so late. His explanation was that the place we were going did not usually begin to warm up until after eleven o'clock at night. "If that was the case, why did you ask me to turn up here as early as nine o'clock," I asked him. He merely laughed it off and said "I hope you are well- loaded, because it could be pretty tough."

"What could be pretty tough?" I asked him partly out of fear and partly out of anxiety. "Nothing serious, old boy, I mean the money," he replied casually. My anxiety grew. "What money?" I asked. Walking jauntily by my side, he dismissed my question with, " You government people like to ask too many questions; enter any office to ask for a simple thing and they start shouting questions at you to drive you away; your Embassy here is the worst of them all." After this, I did not know what to say. I had a secret foreboding that I was walking towards trouble and danger. We walked on in silence.

We turned down a number of streets and presently my friend halted in front of a building. We went to the side of the building and there was a flight of stairs winding down into some subterranean dungeon. He led the way and I followed him down. Already my heart started to beat faster and I started to wonder what adventure or misadventure I had led myself into. We finally arrived at a door. My intrepid partner knocked on the door. The sight of the man who opened it was enough to strike terror into anyone. He had a deep scar on one side of his face, and had only one eye, large and menacing. The place where the other eye should be was covered with a patch. His arms were heavily tattooed and he carried a gun hanging from a holster on his waist.

My stomach turned at these ominous sights. I nudged my friend to tell him to let us beat a retreat, but before I could speak, he had entered and I had to follow him. On entering the room, the sight that greeted my eyes was beyond description. Smoke and fume from cigarettes and marijuana filled the room. I started to cough and my eyes felt as though pepper had been thrown into them. For two or three minutes I could see nothing. The room was dark for it was so dimly lit that you have to squint before you could see anything.

I stood petrified. After some moments, I could discern human figures in various degrees of undress, most of them turning in our direction and staring at us with cold and hostile looks. I knew I should never have allowed this ragamuffin of a friend to drag me

94

into this type of place. He held my hand and led me to a table. He asked me if I had ever tasted a white girl and he pointed at the left corner of the room. Sitting round the bar, there were about half a dozen girls. He explained to me that it was mandatory in the club that we should each send for a girl to entertain us and that they would later give us all the pleasures we wanted.

He beckoned to two of the girls and they joined us at our table. A look at each of the two girls was enough to make me feel like vomiting. Their faces were heavily painted, eye-lashes stretched four inches while they were weighted down with loads of ear-rings and bangles. Their hair was of lurid colours, and it was too obvious that no natural hair could assume such frightful hues. The two girls did not even wait for us to ask what they would drink. They beckoned to the bar and one evil-looking ruffian brought three glasses and announced, "7 pounds please." My friend turned to me and nudged his head in the direction of the evil-looking ruffian. I produced 7 pounds and gave it to him.

Before the man returned to base, the two ladies had signalled for another round of drinks. It was then that I noticed that my good friend pointed up his index finger, signalling a drink for himself. The bill came. "7 pounds please," and my friend turned to me. This went on five times and each time I produced seven pounds. Anger, confusion and disgust, all welled up within me that I had no appetite for any drink. But this did not disturb my friend and the two ladies.

After the sixth round when I had parted with forty-two pounds, I had less than five pounds left. I therefore told my friend to inform the two ladies that it was time to depart, for their love-nest to commence the sexual pleasures for the night. It was then I received another shock. He told me quite calmly that the club rule was, that a client must buy at least seven rounds of drinks before he could take any lady out. I told him about my financial situation, but he merely shrugged his shoulders and said that in that case we had better be going home.

We got up; all the men in the foul den turned their eyes in our direction. The one-eyed man with the scar and gun moved swiftly in our direction. I made hastily for the exit and ran up the steps with all the speed at my command. Back on the street, I breathed God's fresh air as well as freedom. I felt like a man who had just escaped from a den of robbers and everything was like a nightmare to me. My friend took his time in coming out. He ascended the stairs leisurely. He came up to me and to my greatest shock, he started to blame me for ruining all the fun of the evening and that the fun had just begun. I was too full of fury to answer him. I merely headed for the nearest tube station and sat hunched in one corner in the train, brooding over the misadventures of the evening.

Back in the house, I found my wife sitting up, distraught with fear and anxiety. "Where have you been? I rang your office several times and there was no reply," she cried, with tears in her eyes.

"Oh, sweet darling, we were in the office of the High Commissioner. We were preparing an urgent situation report which must get to Nigeria within the next forty-eight hours." With this, I went straight to bed. From her looks I could see that in situations of this nature, women cannot be deceived; they have that natural intuition. She merely sighed and followed me to bed.

TWENTY-ONE

Another three years have rolled by and I have now moved to the Ministry of Finance, as Permanent Secretary. There was a Committee of Administrative officers consisting of the most senior Permanent Secretaries. They were responsible for the postings of all administrative officers in the Civil Service and they also did the promotion exercises. They made recommendations to the Civil Service Commission and in the case of Permanent Secretary promotion, their recommendations went to the Premier. The Head of Civil Service was chairman of these committees.

By and large, it was almost a one-man Committee because, even Permanent Secretaries, no matter how senior, entertained a deep fear and respect for the Head of Civil Service because of his unique position in government and his close intimacy with the Premier. He might recommend to the Premier that a particular Permanent Secretary had outlived his usefulness and should be sent out of the Civil Service. He alone made recommendations to the Premier on the postings of Permanent Secretaries. A Permanent Secretary who was out of favour with him could find himself without a Ministry, and be put in cold storage to vegetate on special duties in the Premier's Office.

For all these considerations, all Permanent Secretaries, while attempting to put up a brave show and speak their minds frankly before the Head of Civil Service, knew when discretion is the better part of valour. They knew when to drop an argument and put on a smiling face and nod appreciatively at whatever the Head of Civil Service decided to do.

At the time I was put up for consideration for the post of Permanent Secretary, I was the most junior and the youngest among the nine officers eligible for promotion. Most of the members of the Committee felt that I was outside the range of consideration and, that the Committee should pick one from among the three most senior officers. The Head of Civil Service took a different view. "Look here, gentlemen, I am not running a rehabilitation home for the old and disabled. I am Head of a Civil Service, whose main aim is efficiency; and I mean efficiency, no matter where I can find it. Alade may be the youngest and the most junior of the nine officers before us, but look at the records. Over the past five or six years he had consistently been rated 'A' in his over-all gradings, while, the others were on the average performance of 'B' and 'C'. You want me to place mediocrity over brilliance and efficiency? No, gentlemen, not when I am still responsible for this Civil Service."

With this, members of the Committee knew that it was no use, indeed, that it was dangerous for them, to pursue the matter further. While some exchanged glances, others looked down at their papers, while one or two turned towards the Chairman and grinned sheepishly to acknowledge his genius and superiority. So, one hot afternoon as I was sweating over the electoral regulations relating to local government elections, my Confidential Secretary came in smiling and blushing from ear to ear. She carried a letter in her hand and wanted to deliver it personally, rather than send it through the messenger, as was the usual practice.

I looked up and saw her smiling at me meaningfully, If anything, it was anger that welled up within me. If this lady was bent on seducing me, surely there is a time and place for everything and not when I was competing with time to complete work on arrangements for the forthcoming local government elections. In any case, I had never been interested in her. As a matter of fact, she made my stomach turn each time I saw her and the feeling which I had for her was one of sympathy and disgust. She was so poorly endowed. Her chest was practically flat, the little breasts she possessed had long taken shelter. My preference was for bosomy girls. Her face was dry and severe while her legs which reminded one of a spider, were inter-twined at various junctions before touching the ground. But on the whole, I preferred it this way, for it kept my mind on my work. A pretty Secretary is a constant source of distraction and temptation, which could rapidly end up in complications and embarrassment.

She carried the letter like a banner and approached me with a knowing smile. I asked her what it was all about. Her answer was that she wanted to be the first to offer me congratulations. "Congratulations on what?" I asked. "Open the letter and read," was her reply. I obeyed and read:

"Dear Alade,

The Premier, acting on the advice of the Civil Service Commission and the Head of the Civil Service has approved your appointment as a Permanent Secretary. Please accept my congratulations."

Signed

Head of Civil Service."

Now, I could not conceal my delight mingled with surprise. I shot up from my seat and hugged her. It was later when I sobered up a bit that two thoughts crossed my mind. How did my Secretary know the contents of the letter? Secondly, how on earth could I have hugged such a caricature of a human being. The answers to the two questions were simple. Secretaries behave like members of a cult. They use their telephones to transmit and circulate pieces of information which they picked from their bosses and were considered hot stuff. As for the second, there can be no other explanations than temporary madness occasioned by over-joy.

Letters and telegrams of congratulations began to pour in. Groups of friends gave parties in my honour, my towns-people resident in town arranged a reception and presented me with an Address and a gold-edge Bible. Back at home, there was a grand reception during which I was reminded to use my new position to bring pipe-borne water and electricity to the town. The Chiefs, who had always deplored my marriage to a girl outside my tribe, urged the paramount ruler to present me with a wife among our native girls who would always remind me of my obligations to my native town.

I thought it necessary that my mode of dressing should reflect my new exalted position. I still recalled what I had learnt in my study of History at the University that, authority is increased by a show of dignity. I therefore went to my bank and withdrew almost my entire savings. With this, I acquired three new suits, two pairs of shoes, half a dozen dressing shirts and some trendy ties.

I had just come out of the bath and was getting dressed for the day's work when my telephone rang. I hate to be disturbed at the last few moments when my heart was set to leave the house and start the day's work. In an angry mood I lifted the receiver and bellowed "Hello, yes?" The caller was one of my colleagues. "Have you heard the news?" he asked me. "What news?" I asked back. And then he said that there had been a military coup in the country. "What does that mean?" I asked him. "It means we are in trouble; the Prime Minister has been kidnapped, two Premiers have been killed; there were shootings in the Army barracks all night."

It was in a state of confusion that I left the house for the office.

Shops were closed, every one fled from the streets in panic. Soldiers were seen patrolling the streets in armoured vehicles. Fear gripped every one. What were all these going to mean? What is Military coup? I had read of it happening in a few African countries, but no one here in Nigeria had ever experienced it.

All the Permanent Secretaries hurried to the office of the Head of Civil Service. There was chaos everywhere. We found him on the telephone to Lagos, trying to find out what was happening and what State governments were expected to do. We felt like a ship at sea without a captain, a compass and indeed, without anything to steer it with. After trying without any success to get through to Lagos, the Head of Civil Service advised us to go back to our various Departments and restore peace and order as much as possible. We should re-assemble at twelve noon when he would have got some information from Lagos.

I returned to my Department in the Ministry of Finance, amidst wild rumours everywhere. It was rumoured that it is an offence to see more than two people standing together on the streets, they would be suspected of plotting against the new military regime; that soldiers patrolling the streets had fired into three groups of people in the city killing five people. We heard that three Ministers and two Permanent Secretaries had been picked up from their homes and had been shot that morning. It was also rumoured that an order had been issued in Lagos, that all Premiers and Permanent Secretaries were to be sent to Kirikiri Maximum prison in Lagos for detention.

Later that morning, all Permanent Secretaries re-assembled in the office of the Head of Civil Service. He appeared nervous and fretful. He announced to us that a Military Governor was to be appointed that morning and would arrive in the State by air later in the day. He directed each of us to go and prepare comprehensive briefs on our Departments so as to brief the new Military Governor. I returned to my office with my mind in a state of turmoil. First, I telephoned my wife and informed her that if she did not see me by the end of the day, she should come and look for me at Kirikiri Maximum prison in Lagos. I told her to look after the children very well. She burst into tears, threw away the telephone and before I knew it, she had arrived in the office. I explained the situation of things to her and handed over my keys and other valuables to her. She left me, sobbing profusely. Then I settled down to prepare a brief on my Ministry.

Late in the afternoon, we were asked to proceed to the airport to meet the new Governor. Only officials were present there. Ministers and other political appointees like chairmen of corporations had all gone into hiding. Indeed, one of them who was my close relation gave me a secret telephone number. He begged me to call him on that number to give him up-to-date information. He kept ringing me almost every hour, to find out if there were any developments. Each time he spoke in whispers. He made himself a nuisance to me all day.

We lined up on the tarmac at the airport as the plane touched down in due course. Everyone was nervous, expecting the worst. As the Governor alighted, he was met by the Commissioner of Police, the Head of the Army Garrison in the city and our Head of Civil Service. There were soldiers everywhere with guns pointed in different directions; some crouched hidden inside the bush, some knelt down around the airport with their guns pointed at the crowd which had gathered to witness the unusual occasion. The new Military Governor took the salute and inspected the guard prepared for him. Then he came straight to us. I said a quick prayer and prepared myself for the worst.

The Head of Civil Service introduced us in turn to the new Military Governor. I could observe that the Governor was doing his utmost to look fierce and intimidating. When the introduction ritual was completed, he walked away to the car which took him to the Government House. Now, we were perplexed as to what to do next. Should we follow him in a convoy to the Government House or should we depart to our different homes. We deliberated on this and took a hurried decision. We would follow the Head of Civil Service. He had entered his car and followed the Military Governor; we too followed.

On reaching the Government House, we all stood sheepishly at the foyer, while our boss, the Head of Civil Service, made a show of being busily engaged giving instructions to the stewards. In the meantime, the Military Governor had disappeared upstairs. Our Head of Civil Service must indeed be a man of courage, for after a short while, he followed the Governor upstairs. No sooner had he gone up than he came down in a hurry and said that we could go that the Governor would meet us next day at ten o'clock.

As I drove into my compound and came out of the car, my little children started shouting "Mummy, Mummy, Daddy is not killed, daddy has come back." Then, they ran back to me and asked, "Daddy, are they still going to kill you? Go and bring out your gun, we will shoot them first and kill all of them." In this anxious state of mind, my family and I ended the day. Things were not made easier when I woke with alarm in the middle of the night and sweating profusely. I had been having an awful dream in which war had broken out and I was being chased by soldiers intent on killing me.

TWENTY-TWO

Next morning, the whole Secretariat was humming with excitement. A military Governor had arrived to rule the State; no more Premier, no more Ministers. Perhaps very soon there also would be no Permanent Secretaries for, there were rumors that they were to be detained, while some of them might even be shot. I spent the morning in amending the brief of my Ministry which would be submitted to the Military Governor.

Ten o'clock came. I first went into the toilet to check on my dress and I took the opportunity to offer a few words of prayer.

All the Permanent Secretaries assembled in the Executive Council Chambers, awaiting the Military Governor. While some remained sullen and silent, some spoke in quiet and subdued voices, a few tried without success to put on a nonchalant look of unconcern, cracking dry jokes. Soldiers with guns cocked on the ready were stationed in the ante-room, while many more were swarming along the corridors. Civil Servants all barricaded themselves behind their doors for fear of what might befall them if they fell foul of the soldiers.

In due course, the door flew open and the Military Governor came in followed by his Aide-de-camp and our Head of Civil Service. We all stood up. He took his seat and asked us to sit. He glared round the room, then he began to speak. "Good Morning, gentlemen; I nearly said Ladies and Gentleman and I quickly remembered that there are no lady Permanent Secretaries." At this joke, some of us laughed nervously. Then he went on. "You have all heard what has happened. Our country is in ruins as a result of mis- government, embezzlement and corruption. We cannot conduct ordinary election without rigging them. We resorted to violence, killing and maiming our fellow citizens. We in the Military cannot continue to look on while the country slides dangerously into ruin and anarchy. The pity of it is that, it is not the common people who are guilty of these crimes. It is the so-called leaders - politicians, Ministers, Chairmen, Permanent Secretaries and even the Judiciary."

At the mention of Permanent Secretaries among the nation's criminals, my heart missed a beat and some of us shuffled in our chairs. At this moment, a soldier came in, gave a smart salute and

went to whisper to the Governor that the Chief Judge had arrived. Should he be told to wait? At this the Governor's eyes flashed fire, "Wait for what?" he cried. "Bring him in." The Chief Judge was ushered in. One could see that although he was trying to put up a dignified composure, he was really nervous and frightened.

The Military Governor wasted no time on preliminaries. He looked straight at the Chief Judge and exclaimed, "Good morning, Chief Judge. No doubt you must be feeling happy for the havoc you have done in this State; or should I say you should be feeling sorry for yourself?" The Chief Judge was now thoroughly unnerved. He managed to whisper in a hoarse voice, "Your Excellency, with great respect, I do not understand you."

Now the Military Governor was really furious. "You do not understand, how can you understand? You can only understand when you are busy delivering judgments to rig elections and turn the state upside down." "Your Excellency," the Chief Judge started, but he was promptly cut short. "Now listen," continued the Governor, "I did not summon you here to engage in arguments with you. I summon you here to sentence you. You have been sentencing people for so long; it is time that you should be sentenced yourself. I give you 48 hours to pack your things and disappear from the Courts. If I see you around after 48 hours, you will have yourself to blame. That is all. Get out."

The Chief Judge was dazed. He turned to go out, his legs wobbling under him. The door had scarcely shut behind him when the Head of Civil Service who was sitting next to the Governor, cleared his throat and said, "Your Excellency, it is not that simple to dismiss a Chief Judge; there are processes and procedures under the Constitution and the Laws..."

The Military Governor did not allow the Head of the Civil Service to complete the sentence, when he cut in and rounded up hotly on him. "Constitution and Laws! Constitution and Laws, my foot! Was there no constitution and laws when you all turned this place to a battle-ground and threw the constitution and laws to the wind! Was there no Constitution and Laws when you started burning houses and people! And you, in particular should take responsibility for the chaos in our country today. You were the Chief Secretary to the Government and the Head of the Civil Service. What advice did you give the Civilian Government when all the evil deeds were being perpetrated? If they did not take your advice, why have you not resigned in protest? Frankly speaking, I think you too should go. I hereby retire you with immediate effect."

There was hushed silence in the room as we all turned to look at the latest victim of the military take-over. He sat still, looking dazed as though he would faint any moment. Some of us shuffled nervously in our seats, not certain whether to plead for him or join him in a protest walk out. In the end, he packed his papers and walked out. Fear gripped the rest of us. I hardly heard the rest of the Governor's address. I could pick out that he was not going to appoint any Commissioners for the moment and that each Permanent Secretary would take charge of his Department and report directly to the Governor. This was followed by a lot of threats issued out in generous doses to each and every one of us in the room, and to the civil servants in general. He picked up his stick and marched out, followed by his ADC.

Two days later, a circular letter went round from the Governor's office, inviting top government officials to a send-off luncheon in honour of the out-going Head of the Civil Service. Some of us were sure that he would decline to turn up in view of the humiliating manner in which he was sent out of the Service. Some said that he ought to attend and take the opportunity to give the Governor the length of his tongue. Some said that if he dared to make such a speech at the luncheon, he would end up in detention.

The day came. Word had gone round that a Military Governor's invitation was indeed a command and no one dared to be absent. And so we trooped into the Government House promptly at one o'clock. There was clearly some nervous tension in the room. No one was sure how best to greet the guest of honour, - the Head of the Civil Service. Should one approach him and express deep sympathy on the fate that had befallen him or should one just say "Good Afternoon Sir?" In the end, nearly all of us adopted the latter course of action. I went up to him as he stood with a glass of fanta in hand, stammered out a "good afternoon, Sir" and hurriedly moved to another part of the room.

Presently, the Military Governor appeared. There was a hushed silence. He picked up a glass of beer from the tray and started moving round, followed by his ADC and the Commissioner of Police. Everyone introduced himself as he came round. There were two or three among us who came from his part of the country and who had been at school with him. These smiled confidently at him and even shared jokes with him. The rest of us peered cautiously at him praying silently to return home safe and sound.

All of a sudden, the Governor turned in his tracks and headed for the dining room. The Protocol Officer had pinned names by the plates to indicate seating position. The Governor, the Battalion Commander, the Commissioner of Police and the Guest of Honour sat at the head of the table. The rest of us took our places. As the lunch drew to a close, the Governor got up and made a speech. He hardly referred to the guest of honour, but dwelt on the sad state of the nation and the determination of the Military to right the wrong. He called for honesty, absolute loyalty and hardwork on the part of all public officers and hinted ominously at the dire consequences awaiting anyone who fell below expectations. He sat down and we all clapped dutifully. Then the Guest of Honor, our erstwhile Head of the Civil Service got up and moved to the microphone to respond to the Governor's speech. He had just said, "Your Excellency," when the Governor signalled to the boys behind him and all of a sudden we heard the strains of the National Anthem. Everybody stood to attention and as it ended, the Governor went out. The Guest of Honour was still holding the microphone as everyone trooped out.

TWENTY-THREE

The Military Governor had directed me to bring him names for appointment to the various Boards of Education. As he said that it was very urgent, I took the lists of names to him at the Government House, after office hours. He was sitting outside on the lawn, surrounded by four or five men, whom I presumed must be his close friends. They were all drinking, chatting and laughing noisily. I knew all of them very well and I had always tried to avoid their company, for they were empty headed and boastful people. Some of them were without any visible means of livelihood, but existed by dubious deals and contracts.

When they saw me appear on the lawn, they exchanged significant winks. I was clutching my files in my hand. I greeted the Military Governor and he invited me to take a chair. A steward came swiftly to my side and asked me what I wanted to drink. I politely declined. Immediately, I became the subject of discussion.

"Mr. Alade, why are you not drinking anything?" said one.

"Don't mind him, he is only pretending; he wants to show the Governor that he is a good boy," answered another. Another one bellowed "then he does not know the Governor; he does not judge you by what you drink, but by your hard-work. What he wants is loyalty and hard work, but you top civil servants are all useless."

Then the Military Governor asked if I had completed the lists. He asked the steward to take the files from me and take them into his office. One of his cronies said, "better be careful, Governor, of the advice these civil servants give you; before you know it they will work towards your destruction. They will appear before you looking pious, humble and honest; it is a lie. They are devils in sheep's clothing." At this, they all laughed uproariously while the steward refilled their glasses of whisky. I got up and bade the Governor good-night. I could still hear the noise of their loud laughter as I entered my car and drove off.

Two weeks later, the Governor prepared a programme for a familiarisation tour of the state. He picked me as the Permanent Secretary to accompany him. I was supposed to function as his chief adviser, prepare his speeches and generally ensure that everything went smoothly. We started off from the Government House. The first port of call was the University, about two hours away.

A mile or two before we entered the town, school children lined both sides of the road, sweating profusely under the heat of the burning sun. I could not help feeling sorry for children of tender age, exposed for so long to the heat of the day. I knew that a good many of them would have had nothing to eat that morning before coming to school. Our convoy drove at break-neck speed past the school children. As there were over twenty cars hurtling away at terrific speed, the poor children could not have been able to identify which car the Governor drove in.

We reached the University hall, where local dignitaries, as well as University dons and students had assembled. My car was about fifteen places behind the Governor's car, according to protocol. Two security cars followed immediately behind the Governor, then a spare car for the Governor. Then there followed two cars occupied by persons who were not government functionaries, but known to be special friends and confidants of the Governor. These were followed by seven cars, each one carrying a State Commissioner. It was after all these, that my car found a place in the queue.

The result of this situation was that when the Governor's car stopped and he came out and was being led to his seat in the Hall, I was still far away behind. When I was finally able to alight from my car, I was forced to sprint a good 400 yards to be at the side of the Governor. The sprinting was absolutely necessary because I was to deliver the opening introductory address, before calling on the Vice-Chancellor to deliver his welcome address to the Governor. Panting and sweating, I hurried to my seat in the front row, my chair had been placed at the far end. I was still trying to catch my breath when the announcement came on the microphone that the Permanent Secretary would now deliver the opening address.

When it came to the turn of the Military Governor to address the gathering, his Private Secretary handed him his speech. It was prepared by me, a product of several hours of careful drafting phrased in choice English Language and calculated to draw applause on every page. The Military Governor rose amidst thunderous clapping and he began:

>Pro-Chancellor,
>Vice-Chancellor,
>You Highnesses,
>Members of the University Council,
>Members of Senate,

Your Excellencies,
Members of the Diplomatic corps,
My Lords, Temporal and Spiritual,
Commissioner of Police,
Honourable Commissioners,
Staff and Students,
Distinguished Guests,
Ladies and Gentlemen.

I had spent several days diligently and labouriously preparing the Governor's speech. I had taken the pains to visit the University library to check on certain references and I had made sure that my quotations from various authors and scholars were accurate. I wanted to show the academic world that they did not hold the monopoly of intelligence and academic excellence, and that there were brilliant men and first class brains in the Civil Service. There was perfect silence as eyes and ears opened wide in excitement and great expectations.

To my greatest distress, the Governor started stumbling through each page, pausing at wrong places and mis-pronouncing several words. He thoroughly massacred the speech and it was a complete disaster. I had never been so upset in all my life. Of course, at the end of the ceremony, sycophants and favour-seekers rushed round to congratulate the Governor on the brilliant speech and the wonderful delivery.

TWENTY-FOUR

It is my habit to bring work home from the office. I usually go to bed around ten o'clock and would be up about four o'clock in the morning. Then I would go into my study and work on my office papers and files until seven o'clock. Thereafter, I would go for my bath, get dressed, have some breakfast and leave for the office, arriving there at about 8 a.m.; that is thirty minutes after the official opening hours.

On this particular morning, I reached the Secretariat entrance at about 8.15 a.m. and found the gate locked. Four armed soldiers were standing by. There was a large collection of civil servants who had been arrested and detained at the gate by the soldiers. They were not allowed to proceed to their various departments.

As I reached the gate, one of the soldiers ordered me out of my car and asked if I was a civil servant. It quickly dawned on me that the civil servants detained at the gate were late-comers. I thought very fast. Putting on a look of outraged dignity, I told the soldier that I am not a civil servant, but a businessman and that I had an appointment at the Ministry of Industries. With this explanation, the soldier opened the gate and I drove in and went to my office.

About an hour later, the Military Governor appeared on the scene and descended on the late-comers who were an assortment of officials of all grades. Among them were Permanent Secretaries, and Heads of Departments. There were also junior officials, down to clerks and messengers. They were all lined up together. Then the Military Governor admonished them. He called them all sorts of names and poured every invective of abuse on them. When he had exhausted his arsenal of abuses and threats, he ordered the soldiers to drill them for an hour, before they were allowed to go to their various offices.

Now the average Nigerian soldier is known for his sadistic tendencies, the joy of subjecting his fellowmen to suffering and harassment. The Military Governor had given the four soldiers the license they had always dreamed about. With great glee, they set off to work on the luckless civil servants. They were asked to hold their ears and jump up; they were made to leap-frog. Then came running when the soldiers, with lash in hand, chased the civil servants round and round the field. Quite a number got some strokes of the cane.

Before the exercise ended, there were casualties; a few ladies and some pot-bellied men collapsed, drenched with sweat. Two or three were rushed to the hospital. The more the casualties littered the field, the more the soldiers gloated and laughed, shouting "these bloody civilians."

Later in the day, the Permanent Secretaries and other Heads of Department met to review the events of the day. We decided to lodge a strong protest to the Military Governor. It was unfair and unjust for senior civil servants who put in several hours of work in their private time, to be subjected to humiliation, merely because they were late to work. Some of us, after closing at the end of the day, returned to the office later in the evening and worked till late. Some took their files home and worked for long hours into the night. We decided to tell the Governor that matters of punctuality should be left to each Department to deal with. The Head of each Department should decide ways of ensuring discipline among the junior workers.

We had decided to march to the Governor, all of us. Later, we considered that the Military mind might misconstrue this as rebellion or conspiracy. In the end, we left matters in the hands of the Head of the Civil Service, to make our feelings known to the Governor. We waited for three weeks, and kept reminding him at the weekly meetings of Permanent Secretaries. Each time, the matter was raised, the Head of Service would merely nod and say "Oh, yes, I will see the Governor." Each time, we winked to one another and exchanged glances. In the end we decided that discretion was the better part of valour and we stopped reminding him. Sometimes there is safety in silence.

TWENTY-FIVE

And so it happened that one fine morning, there were strong rumours flying around that the Military Governor was to be posted back to the barracks. A good many of us were happy at the news. We were fed up with his excesses. All-night parties with his cronies, where drinks and women were supplied in abundance. Indeed the regular supply of women and the changing of those of them not considered pleasurable, had been developed into a great assignment. There were officials and other close associates of the Governor, whose duty it was to scout round the city and neighbouring towns and States to collect the women. Official cars and drivers were permanently assigned for the task.

We had more reasons to rejoice at the impending departure of the Governor. A class of individuals had grown up in the State, who considered themselves above the law of the land and the normal etiquette of decent human behaviour. They wanted everyone to know, that they were very close to the Military Governor and, that a little whisper by them to the Governor could cost you your job or even your freedom. They were arrogant and most insolent. The worst part of it was that this class of persons was not limited to private citizens. There were civil servants of relatively junior grades who constituted a law unto themselves. They turned up in the office when they like and sometimes were absent from work for several days without permission. The Head of Department dared not query them.

Again, some of us were worried at the speed at which ill-advised and ill-digested schemes and projects were being implemented. A new vocabulary term had entered the public service. Everyday things had to be carried out with immediate effect. "Get me the Permanent Secretary, Ministry of Industries on the phone." "Please hold on for the Military Governor." A few moments later, "Is that the Permanent Secretary?" "Yes, Sir, Good morning, your Excellency."

"I told you two days ago to conclude negotiation on the Oil Palm project and get papers ready for the Agreement to be signed..."

"Yes, Your Excellency, but..."

"But what? Instead of carrying out my instructions you sent me several pages of lengthy sermon. Do you think I am here to waste

113

my precious time reading the rubbish people like you write?"

"But, Your Excellency..."

"Shut up and listen. I want that Agreement signed with immediate effect." With this the Governor banged the telephone.

Very soon, rumors crystallised into fact. The Military Governor was indeed, returning to the barracks. His close associates and cronies became crest-fallen. There was a look of despondency on their faces and they became much less insolent and arrogant. Indeed, as I was descending the steps of the Government House, I sighted one of them and I tried to avoid him. To my surprise, I heard his voice:

"Good Morning, Sir," I did not answer nor look at his direction. He moved nearer and repeated the salutation. It was then that I stopped and gave him a cold but polite greeting, hoping to get him off my back. But he was not to be shaken off so easily:

" I have always wanted to come and visit you in the house, but I am always on the move. I will certainly come this next week-end."

I replied that it was very kind of him and I entered my car and drove off.

True enough, the vile creature called at my house the following week-end. I was away at the time, but my wife received him.

"I am Chief Foluso, a friend of your husband," he announced to my wife.

"Your husband, Mr. Alade, and I have been very close for years. It is my constant travelling on business that has prevented me from visiting you." My wife offered him drinks and he spread out himself and felt entirely at home. He went on to tell my wife:

"Your husband is a wonderful man; he is a pride to us. If we have two of his type in Government service, this country would have been a wonderful country." When my wife reported the visit to me, and wondered why she was seeing for the first time someone who described himself as my close friend. I explained to her that he was one of the rats trying to escape and find a new abode before the ship sink.

The news of the intending departure of the Governor now filled the air. There were rumours that he was pulling all the wires to prevent his being posted away. Traditional rulers were said to be making preparations to lead a delegation to the Head of State to plead that the Governor should be left alone. Writers were hired to shout in the newspapers that it was not in the interest of the state to change a Governor who had come to understand the people so well and the people loved him and had confidence in him. But as most of us knew, the people were joyous and felt a sense of relief to hear that the Governor was going. So much were his excesses. Gossip even had it that the Governor had resorted to native herbalists and that cows were being buried alive daily. As if to confirm the truth of this gossip, the Governor now kept disappearing to his hometown about twice every week.

But it had become inevitable that he must go. A circular went round that each Department must submit a list of projects in the pipe-line and those earmarked for the future. Not long after, another circular announced a grand farewell tour of the Governor. An itinerary was attached to the Circular. The farewell tour was to last for four whole weeks, during which the Governor would stop in fifty-two towns to address the communities in each place.

Not only was he going to address the various communities, but he was going to lay the foundation stone of one thing or the other in each place. Hospitals, Secondary schools, Civic Centres, Maternity Centres, Roads, Electricity and Water supplies were not left out. At various places, announcements were to be made that the road linking the communities with the outside world would be tarred with immediate effect.

And so, one fine morning, the fare-well tour took off from the Government House. In all, there were thirty-two motor vehicles in the convoy. Security, Protocol, State Commissioners, Permanent Secretaries, Television crew, Information officials, Hanger on and so forth. At each stopping place, it was a carnival. Hunters lined the road firing their dane guns, half-naked maidens held white horse-tails and wiggled their bottoms. Of course, as usual, school children had lined the route, sweating profusely and looking absolutely miserable.

When everyone had been seated, the Community leader rose and went to the microphone. First, he tapped it several times to make sure that the microphone was functioning. Then he followed this by blowing air into the microphone. When he was finally satisfied that the microphone was in good working condition, he started clearing his throat. This went on again for another couple of minutes, until finally he croaked out:

"An Address, presented by the Entire community of Loba Community, to His Excellency, Colonel Henry Talabi, on the occasion of his farewell visit to Loba.

Your Excellency, Today is a red letter day in the history of our famous town. Like the Biblical Moses, who led the children of Israel out of bondage, you have come today to rescue us from disease and poverty. Today, you are laying the foundation stone of a hospital in our town. From time immemorial, we have suffered and prayed that the day will come when God will send a deliverer. Your name will for ever be written in letters of gold, generations unborn will remember you with gratitude. Farewell, our beloved Governor, Adieu, our wonderful Saviour."

Then there followed cultural dances staged by various groups, each one singing the praises of the Governor, extolling his incomparable virtues. By now, the Governor was gratified beyond belief. When it was time for him to address the gathering, he threw away the speech which had been prepared for him and told the gathering that he was not going to read what the civil servants wanted him to say. He said that he wanted to talk to them as his own people. At this statement there was clapping and loud ovation, while the congregation eyed the civil servants present with hatred and mistrust. The Military Governor continued:

My dear People,

We have remained a backward state for too long and the time has come to put an end to this and move forward on the road to civilization. You will all be interested to know that during the course of this month, I shall be performing in 38 other places the sort of ceremony which I am going to undertake here this morning. Today, I am going to lay the foundation stone of a hospital for you. In 38 other places, I will perform similar ceremony for electricity, water-supply, secondary schools, roads and so forth."

Again, there was deafening ovation. It took quite some time to quiet the people down. After this, a small procession led to the site of the foundation laying ceremony. Cameramen, Television crew, the Press, all sped towards the scene. Then we all returned to the Hall for the Vote of Thanks to the Governor. Another member of the community, said to be secretary of the town's Progressive Association, stepped forward. It was obvious that he was barely literate.

"Your Majesty," he shouted and everyone roared with laughter of derision. This put the poor man in a state of absolute confusion. He made another attempt: "My Lord," again there was another

116

outburst of laughter. He was being booed and heckled, all this got him all the more confused.

At this juncture, the community leader signalled to a lady sitting in the front row. She stepped up to the dais bearing a parcel in her hands. Her shape and figure arrested my attention. Her fair complexion, shapely legs and a round face tipped by a small nose, she was indeed a vision of beauty. The breasts bubbled as she walked, while the nipples shone faintly underneath the blouse. She stepped on to the stage where the secretary of the community was still looking round sheepishly, and in a thin and quivering voice, she said into the microphone:

"On behalf of the Chiefs and entire community of Loba town, I present your Excellency with this gift in appreciation of all you have done for us. We wish you happiness and success in the future." She then stepped to the Governor to present him with the gift. The Governor took it and held out his hand to shake the lady. I could not help noticing that the Governor held her hand longer than was necessary. I felt a pang of jealousy.

So for the next month, we travelled around in a long convoy. The scenario was the same - welcome address, laying foundation stone, cultural displays, vote of thanks, farewell gift. Each morning before we set out, the Governor assembled all the day's news-papers and scanned through to see how the press reported the news of his tour. It was easy to observe a look of pleasure on his face when he saw his pictures and read the praises showered on him the previous day.

Three weeks before the commencement of the farewell tour, the Ministry of Information had been ordered to prepare brochures. One booklet should contain the Military Governor's speeches since his assumption of office in the State. Another publication should depict the Governor's five years activities in pictures. Yet a third publication should contain a well-doctored write up, to be cap-tioned "Five Years of Progress." Each of the three publications was to be printed in several thousands of copies.

The Ministry of Information complained that it had no vote in its budget from which to undertake such a huge expenditure, estimated at about N150,000. The Ministry, applied to the Ministry of Finance for release of funds to meet the unexpected expenditure. That Ministry was aghast at the idea of spending such a colossal sum on such unproductive ventures, especially, when half a million naira had earlier been ordered to be released to cover expenses connected with the farewell ceremonies. There was to be a state dinner bringing in dignitaries from all over the State; there was to be a gala night when dancers, musicians and entertainers were to be transported to the State capital. They would have to be housed and fed and paid incidental expenses.

In short, the Ministry of Finance refused to release any more money, unless specifically ordered to do so by the Governor. And so the matter went to the Military Governor. He bellowed with rage and sent for the Commissioner and the Permanent Secretary in the Ministry of Finance. He accused them of subversion and sabotage. The Commissioner disowned any knowledge of the matter and pleaded that the Permanent Secretary did not bring the matter to his attention. Whereupon, the Governor unleashed his venom on the Permanent Secretary:

'I know you are one of those who are happy that I am going away, but before I go I will show you that I am still the Military Governor. You civil servants are all the same, only eye- service, no loyalty. I will make you an example to people of your type. You are hereby suspended with no pay, with immediate effect. I will decide your fate later. If you think because I am going away you are beyond my discipline, you are wrong."

Three weeks later, when the farewell tour took off, one of the vans in the convoy was loaded with several thousands copies of

Five years of Progress
Military Governor's 5-years activities in pictures
5 years Memorable speeches of the Governor.

They were all to be distributed free at each stopping place. As I watched the publications being distributed, I wondered if any of the recipients realised that the Governor never wrote a single line in any of the publications. Nor did he even see a good many of the speeches until they were handed to him for delivery.

TWENTY-SIX

Circular Letter,

Office of the Secretary
to the Military Government,
Military Governor's Office.

The Military Governor will be departing from the State on Thursday. All Permanent Secretaries, Chairmen of Statutory Boards and Corporations, Heads of non-Ministerial Departments, should assemble at the Government House to bid His Excellency farewell.

Signed:.......................
for Secretary to the Military
Government.

A few of those who had suffered various forms of humiliation, injustice or persecution at the hands of the Governor tore the circular into pieces and threw it into their waste - paper basket. There was nothing more he could do to them. Some even swore that sooner or later he would retire from the Army and they would meet as man to man, fellow Nigerians. Then they would let him know precisely what they thought of him. After all, no condition is permanent.

To All Permanent Secretaries,
All Chairmen of Statutory,
Board and Corporations,
Heads of non-Ministerial,
Departments.

ARRIVAL OF THE NEW MILITARY GOVERNOR

The new Military Governor, Lt. Col. Andrew Folude, will be arriving in the State next Monday, all officials and public functionaries named above are to assemble at the Airport at one o'clock p.m. to welcome His Excellency, the Military Governor.

2. The top Traditional Rulers are being notified separately.

No sooner had this second circular letter been issued, when the Secretary to the Military Government saw it, he was extremely angry and he sent for the Assistant Secretary who sent out the Circular.

"All this time that you have been in the Civil Service, you do not know how to write official correspondence." The S.M.G. opened up his anger on the Assistant Secretary, "You think you can write as though you are addressing your local association?" The Assistant Secretary was bewildered. He was about to stammer his excuses, when the S.M.G. went on:

"You mean you haven't known that when you write official correspondence, you must indicate that you have been properly directed to do so? Now get out and cancel your Circular and issue a proper one before the end of the day."

I was not very surprised when towards closing time, I opened a letter urgently delivered by my messenger and read:

"I am directed, to refer to my earlier Circular letter on the above subject and to cancel the said letter. I am further directed, to inform the functionaries named in my earlier Circular, that the new Military Governor, Lt. Col. Andrew Folude, will be arriving in the State next Monday. I am to say, that the functionaries and officials listed in my earlier circular should assemble at the Airport at one o'clock p.m., to welcome His Excellency, the Military Governor.

2. I am further directed to add that top traditional rulers are being notified separately.

Signed: ....
for Secretary to the Military
Government."

"I am directed," I said within me. For as long as I am in this career, I will always be directed. I packed my papers and stood up to go home for the day. I said aloud to myself, "I am directed to say that it is time for me to go home. I am further directed to remember to call at the Supermarket on my way home; I am to add that I must not forget that my car is due for servicing."

The Civil Service is full of many pit-falls and treacherous pot-holes which can trip the unwary young official. It will be in his own interest to study carefully the hints which are listed down here, golden advice distilled from many years of civil service experience.

Before embarking to put into practice the advice in this chapter, it is necessary to sound a note of warning. Just as there are certain drugs which can only be taken after meals and never on empty stomach, so also the hints of golden advice given here should be used only after the civil servant aspiring to the top has first ensured that he is fully equipped with the following:

(a) Sound basic educational qualification;
(b) Efficiency of the first rate;
(c) Undoubted integrity;
(d) Ability to apply tireless energy and be very industrious;
(e) Absolute and transparent honesty;
(f) Unflinching patriotism;
(g) Devotion to duty;
(h) Ability to get on well with colleagues, both senior and junior;
(i) An equable and pleasant disposition and temperament.

Now subject yourself to a critical and impartial self-examination in order to ascertain that you are adequately equipped with all the nine attributes listed above. If you are satisfied that you pass all the nine tests, then you can smile to yourself because you are now standing right in front of the door to success and you have the key in your hands.

But lo and behold! You still require some other essentials, which alone can turn the key you are holding when you insert it into the door. Until then, the door to success will not yield for you to enter. These essentials are of a secret nature and can only be revealed to the initiated. The rites of initiation are contained in a secret document which you have to obtain on application. Prospective candidates under 18 years of age and those over 60 years need not apply. We will now proceed to reveal these essentials on the assumption that you are already initiated. Here we go:

1.   Drop vague hints that you are related to the Head of the Civil Service, and that your mother is a senior sister to the wife of the Head of State. Mention casually some incident which took place while you were having lunch with the Head of State the previous week-end.

2.   Put on continual air of confidence, especially during official meetings with the Head of Civil Service, the Governor or the Head of State. This attribute is particularly essential in a military regime where the soldier-ruler, fresh from the barracks, knows next to nothing about government and public administration. When he presides over meetings, he has no clue as to what is being discussed and so he keeps studying the faces of those before him, and looks from mouth to mouth to see who is most forceful in argument. In such a situation, you must make sure that you out-talk every other person at the meeting. If necessary, bang your fist on the table and shake your index finger at the face of your opposing colleague. The Military ruler will not fail to notice you and will later send for you and make you his close adviser. The door of success is now thrown open and you are on your way to the top.

3   Be smart and neat in your dress. Again, this is particularly essential in a military regime. Soldiers, by training and habit, are smart and neat in their uniforms, with belt and shoes polished to reflect like a mirror. They therefore have a practised eye for smartness and neatness and will look fondly at any official who is habitually well-dressed. Therefore, to get the door of success open to you, avoid incongruous dressing like brown jacket on top of green trousers or brown shoes worn under a dark suit.

4.   Avoid, like the plague, becoming familiar with your boss's wife. She and her husband have not been on speaking terms for years and they live together merely to keep up appearances. Any kind words from her about you to her husband will spell your ruin. Since you know that your boss has an unhappy marital life, make sure whenever social occasions bring you together, to speak most disparagingly about wives and married women. These words will warm the heart of your boss towards you and he will soon be confiding in you, unlocking his heart to pour out the sorrows of his

domestic life.

When relationship between you and your boss get to this intimate stage, you are definitely on your way to the top. You must now seize the opportunity of the moment to strike while the iron is hot. As he pours out his heart to you, you must do your best to look sympathetic. When he has finished, you must assure him that his wife has wronged him and that he has suffered long enough without just cause. He will then turn to you expecting a possible solution to his problem. Now is your chance. Do not miss it. Pretend to be lost in thought for a few seconds, then sigh and say, "Sir, I praise you for having endured so much in the hands of an ungrateful wife, but you cannot go on like this. Life is too short to spend it all in misery. Sir, you must now break free and enjoy yourself...."

Immediately your boss hears this, the idea of breaking free and enjoying himself will fill him with rapturous hopes and expectations. He will then turn to you and say mournfully, "But how? Divorce is out of it for it will create a scandal which a man in my position cannot afford."

Then with great respect and a show of sympathy you will answer, "Of course, Sir, I can understand; divorce is out of the question; I will never advise it for a man like you whom we all respect and admire."

As you have already whetted his curiosity, he will shyly ask you, "What is your solution then, Alabi?" Now is your chance to enter the realms of success and soar to the top. Respectfully clearing your throat, pretending to be half afraid, you will now advance your solution which, in fact, is your own avenue to the top:

"Sir," you will begin, "this life is too short for anyone to live a life of misery, especially someone like you, Sir, who work so hard from morning till night every day. We all talk about you all the time in the Office and prayed we could be half as industrious and efficient as you. If you will forgive me, Sir, for taking such liberties. The solution is for you to take a mistress who will be available all the time to cheer you, comfort you and make you forget all your cares and sorrows. As I say, sir, please forgive me for venturing to make such a suggestion but I am one of your secret admirers and we don't ever want to see you unhappy."

Now watch your boss; you will see his eyes light up and twinkle. He is already savouring the delights that lie in store for him. But

123

he would not want you to see that he is excited. And so, he will say very casually "I cannot think of anyone whom I can approach, even if I do, where do I take her? It will be too risky to book rooms in the hotels?" Here comes your chance to demonstrate your love and concern for your boss. You will now say to him, "Sir, these are no problems at all. I know one or two sales girls who can be absolutely trusted to be discreet. As for the meeting place, I have a nice flat in a quiet area. Once I know the day and time you are coming, I will inform the lady and I will leave the key of the flat under the door-mat."

When the plan gets going, there are many side-benefits for you to reap besides accelerated promotion to the top. Some of these side benefits are:

(a)   You will sometimes return to your flat to find that your boss and his mistress left behind half a bottle of beer, biscuits, or one or two bottles of wine. This is your own commission.

(b)   Unknown to your boss the lady in question now becomes your mistress too, and at no cost to yourself. The boss is spending loads of money on her and as she does not wish to lose this source of wealth, she will gladly take you on at no cost to yourself.

(c)   She will very soon be a sure and effective instrument to get for you whatever you want officially from the boss - promotion, overseas study course, a larger and more comfortable office accommodation, the use of official cars and drivers and a host of other perquisites, which would have been denied to you or cost you a lot of sweat to obtain.

(d)   The lady will pass on to you a good slice of the goodies coming from your boss. The reason is obvious; you are by far a better lover; you are far younger than the boss and therefore, perform with far greater efficiency in bed than your boss who, after a most tiresome day, comes to the flat merely to fall asleep each time. Very often, the good lady out of anger and frustration will wake him up and tell him to go home. He will quietly get up, hand over a wad of money to her, kiss her and bid her good-bye. The lady will now itch for you to come back and give her all the joys and satisfaction she had missed from your boss. At the climax of the enjoyment, she will hold you tight and scream out, "Take all the money he gave me, take it, take it, oh my God, take it all. It is all yours! I am all yours . . ."

(e)   Your boss will soon discover that your bedding, bedsheets, pillow-slips etc. are below his dignity and will order half a dozen sheets etc. for use in your flat. They have become your property.

(f)   You will occasionally, not too frequently, drop gentle hints to your boss that very soon the flat may not be available because the landlord is threatening to evict you for non-payment of outstanding rents. Put on a penitent look and apologise profusely for the unpleasant situation caused by the fact that you had to spend a lot of money on your sick mother; assure him that you will find some way to pay up the outstanding rent. And presto! What do you know? Your telephone will ring and your boss's secretary will say that he wants to see you immediately.

"Ah, yes Alabi, what you mentioned to me yesterday; how much rent are you owing."

You will then cough, appear embarrassed and say, "Not to worry, Sir, I have already approached one or two friends who promised to see what they can do to give me a loan to clear the 200 Naira arrears." The boss pulls out his drawers and hands 200 Naira to you." No, Sir , please Sir, I won't dream of bothering you with my personal problems," Still, you take it, thank him profusely and hurry out of his office. That is "bread" to cushion you for some time!

(5) Just as a military regime requires its own tactics and strategy to get the soldiers, so does a civilian regime requires its own tactics, if you wish to get to the top very fast. Here are few useful hints in a civilian regime. Always remember that they like to think that they are nationalists. This spirit of nationalism extends to dress as well as food and often to women. Therefore, once the military hands over to the civilians, hang up all your suits and ties and change to native dresses for office work. You must, of course, keep a close ear to your radio. Once you hear that a coup has taken place and the soldiers have taken over government, rush home by the quickest route and dust up your suits. Soldiers do not take kindly to officials who are not smartly dressed.

(6) When in the presence of your civilian political bosses - Commissioners, Minister, Premier or President- use every opportunity to sneer at the opposition party and speak disparagingly of them. Very soon, it will become a common topic in government political circle that you are a loyal civil servant and should be given

the highest promotion. Of course, you must remember to put your gear in reverse and sing a different tune if the opposition party comes into power after elections. This is the whole idea of a civil servant being loyal to the government of the day and since your loyalty cancels itself out, you have observed the sacred principle' of political neutrality.

(7) The final hint that I am about to give is the most important of all. Write it in your heart and say it with your prayers day and night. The golden hint is keep clear of diseases that incapacitate and prevent you from performing efficiently. Malaria, colds and the like can be taken in one's strides. But run like mad man when you hear of maladies like hypertension, sickle cell, ulcer of the stomach, cancer. If any of these monster pursue you and catch up with you, then you need not bother to read this last chapter. Instead, sit up and support your back with pillows on your sick bed and begin to calculate your retirement benefits. Then write up your will and put in your retirement papers in time, to allow for a befitting send-off party for you before the bell tolls.

TWENTY-SEVEN

AFTER CIVIL SERVICE - WHAT NEXT?

From a young aspiring civil servant bristling with energy and enthusiasm, you gradually progress through various stages, gathering experience all along, some pleasant and some not too pleasant. Today you are worried about promotion, tomorrow it is posting and transfer. You have been married and your wife - God help you! - has been a source of happiness or misery to you. Whichever be the case, you cannot help it and the children have all been arriving. You look at yourself in the mirror one fine day and notice not only grey hairs sprouting indiscriminatingly all over your head, but also that a lot of hair has mysteriously disappeared from a prominent part of the head.

You sigh and sit down to brood for a while. All sorts of debts are hanging like a millstone round your neck. You are yet to complete the loan repayments on your car; you are falling in arrears on the mortgage loan on the house you are about to complete. In the meantime, the funeral of your father-in-law is approaching and you are expected to produce the cow and the drinks for the occasion. You sigh again, would the bank be willing to grant you more accommodation to meet the funeral expenses?

Just then, the bell rings and you are startled out of your sober thoughts. It is the postman delivering some letters. The very first letter you open contains shattering news, that a storm which raged a few days ago, had blown off the roof of your father's house and the old man had since fallen ill and requires medical attention. You are about to take another deep sigh when your daughter rushes. She informs you that the Principal has announced in the school that examinations begin next Monday, unless she brings N105 to cover examination fees, development levy and school bus levy, she will not be allowed to sit for the examinations.

It never rains, but pours, you say silently inside you. As you attempt to stand up from your chair, a sharp pain stabs you in the joints. You remember that you have had a bad attack of arthritis, which has made life very miserable for you. You get up painfully and prepare to go to work. As you reach the office, the first document that catches your eyes is an official circular. Your first reaction is to throw it aside, but merely for curiosity you decide to glance through it. And then, O Horror of Horrors! Alas!

The Circular reads:

As part of government measures to re-organise the civil service and make it more efficient and productive, civil servants who fall under the following categories are to retire with immediate effect:

(i) All those who are 60 years of age and above;

(ii) All those who have served for up to 35 years or more, including years spent in teaching, clerical and other services;

(iii) All those certified through annual assessment reports and other authoritative sources to suffer from

(a) Inefficiency

(b) Declining productivity

(c) Doubtful probity

(d) Ill health

(e) Old age.

"From records and reports available on you, you are therefore directed to retire with immediate effect. Please hand over all government property in your possession to the Secretary for Finance and Administration in your department. Your retirement benefits and any other entitlements will be settled after your indebtedness to government, if any, has been computed."

Now, you sink with your back hunched in your seat, while cold perspiration begins to trickle down your back. If you are the type with a religious turn of mind, the hymn for the family devotion that evening will be either,

When sorrows like a river attend my ways

When sorrows like sea billows roll

Whatever my lot, thou has taught me to say

It is well with my soul.

Or perhaps,

From every stormy wind that blows

From every swelling tide of woe

There is a calm, a sure retreat

It is found beneath the mercy seat.

But your thoughts return to the present moment. After all, where was the sure retreat and the mercy seat when all these misfortunes started to rain down on you? Lost in these thoughts, you were not aware that your door had opened quietly and a bunch of your subordinate officials stand, nervously looking at you and looking at one another. You lifted up your eyes and said, "Yes, what is it?" They all looked at the oldest one among them, who is your Senior Accounts Officer. He gave a nervous cough, cleared his throat and squeaked, "Sorry, Sir, about what happened."

Now, you cannot allow dignity to suffer, even at the point of exit. And so you force a smile and say, "Very kind of you all, very kind indeed; actually I have myself been planning to go and I am glad this has come." They all file out, while the two female members could be seen wiping their eyes.

Now is the time to tidy your table, pick up your personal effects and prepare handing-over notes for whosoever will take over your desk. Having dictated your handing-over notes, you find that there is precious little more you can do for the rest of the day. It is best to go home and come back the next day to sign the notes and do a formal farewell to your staff.

You arrive home shortly after noon. Your wife is surprised to see you home at this time of the day. Have you forgotten something? You need some refreshment? Of course, women are gifted with great intuition. Even though you try to put on a care-free and nonchalant attitude, she could smell a rat. She gets up and stands by you, her eyes wide with apprehension. Finally, you break the news to her.

Unfortunately for you, you have not been blessed with a sympathetic and understanding wife. All your life, she had been a thorn in your flesh, for ever nagging at you, for ever exploding with quarrel at the slightest argument. Now is the grand opportunity of a lifetime.

"Under which category have you now been dismissed?" She asks,

"I am not dismissed, dear, I am only retired..."

"What difference does it make? You keep on deceiving yourself. My God, that my life should come to end up in shame and disgrace! I dare not show my face in the public. Everybody will be laughing at me. So this is what you have now made of our lives and the lives of our four children. All their mates will be laughing at them in school..."

"But, my dear, retirement is not the end of the world. After all, it is certain I must leave the civil service sooner or later, whether I like it or not. So, now that it has come, I have no regrets..."

"Hear him! you have no regrets! You stand there and shamelessly tell me that you have no regrets? Is this the way Mr. Oluwole left the service? Is this the way Mr. Akande left? Were they not given a rousing send-off party to which all the notables in the society were invited? My God, to think that I would wake up one day and find myself tied to a man dismissed for inefficiency, doubtful probity, declining productivity and who knows, perhaps theft and embezzlement! Oh, my God, what have I done to earn such misfortune and disgrace in my life! What have I done? People warned me at the time not to follow this man. Now here I am being dragged into shame and disgrace..."

This is one of those times that try a man's soul. You come home to find peace and solace but instead, you are faced with antagonism. What do you do? Get up in fury and beat your wife up mercilessly? Get back into your car and drive out? To where? Beating her will only make matters worse. The noise will attract neighbours. Besides, at the end of the beating what have you achieved? You are left panting and exhausted, with your shirt torn and your blood pressure the worse for it. You are lucky if you have not finished up with a black eye and swollen lips.

And so with the wife beyond the pale of reasoning, with the thought of beating her totally out of the question and with the idea of disappearing temporarily out of the house impracticable, you are left with only one option - go into your bedroom, lock yourself up and lie down for a while. Invariably, your mind will be occupied with the questions "What do I do next? Where do I go from here?" This is the most immediate problem for you to tackle.

If you are fortunate to be a professional - Engineer, Medical doctor, Architect, Lawyer, Accountant - then thank your lucky star for the day that you chose science subjects in your secondary school and you pursued them to the University to give you a profession. For you therefore, your problem is light. Simply look for some suitable accommodation in town, make a fancy sign-board to advertise your profession and stick it in front of the place. Get a table and a chair for yourself, and three or four chairs for your prospective customers. Hang around the place, putting on a smiling face and greeting everybody cheerfully. Very soon customers will begin to trickle in and you are in business.

Within a short time, you will be able to gloat with satisfaction that you have lost no income by being thrown out of government employment. After all, upon being retired and having put in over thirty years in government service, you are entitled to not less than seventy percent of your last salary as pension. All you need to make up your salary in government is thirty percent. Therefore, no matter how indolent you are at your new business, and no matter how perfunctory you attend to the business, you will make more than the thirty percent required to make up your former income. You can afford to sit back, put your feet on a stool with a glass of whisky in your hand and reflect that your being thrown out of government was a blessing in disguise. It is government which has lost, and not you.

Indeed you may well find that the blessing of retirement are pouring in so much that in no time you have become a very wealthy man. With your years of experience in government, you should know how to corner government jobs and contracts if, you are a lawyer, an architect, an accountant or an engineer. The Corporations and government-owned companies should be in your pocket. Before long, you discard your old civil service car and cruise around in a Mercedes Benz 280, the envy of all government officials. You can now swing into big social circles and contest the Chairmanship of the District Rotary Club. You go into you local church and volunteer to be Chief Organiser at the next Harvest festival. O Happy Day! Your only regret is that you should have got out of the civil service long ago.

But it is not all those who are thrown out of government who sing O Happy Day. For the great majority, it is a life of misery or even of early death. Not all government officials are Engineers or Medical Doctors. There are those who have risen through the ranks and who have very limited educational background. There are those who entered government service with a degree in the liberal arts - History, English, Philosophy, Political Science. It is to these two categories of retired government officials that this chapter is mainly addressed. It is they who wake up the morning after retirement and sit downcast, hunched in a chair and keep asking themselves 'What do I do now? Where do I go from here? How do I keep body and soul together with the load of family responsibility?'

The problem becomes compounded if you have been forcibly retired. You feel a stigma attached to you, you experience a sense of shame. As you enter the supermarket, the bookshop or the post office, you can sense people turning their heads in your direction, some regarding you with sympathy while some openly jeer and laugh at you. You hastily beat a retreat and rush out like some social leper. For a full month after the retirement, your house is full of sympathisers day and night, commiserating with you over your misfortune. Any casual visitor entering the house would have thought that you had been bereaved and had lost your wife or one of your children.

Indeed, your social problem becomes yet more compounded if you have made some enemies in the public service during your tenure of office. It may be some officials who thought you had unjustifiably denied them of promotion, or it may be some against whom you have had to apply disciplinary sanctions for one lapse or the other. Now is their time to gloat and rejoice over your misfortune. Some will do this discreetly, while some boorish ones will sneer at you to your face and dare you now to touch them. You have indeed hit one of those times that try men's souls.

The question which you will keep asking yourself is - Where do I go from here? What work am I to do next? And you have to answer these questions pretty fast not only to find the wherewithal to meet your financial responsibilities, but more importantly, to save you from premature death. For it is common knowledge that anyone who suddenly becomes inactive after many years of daily hard work, will find that his body disintegrates fast, and very soon body and soul will come to the end of life's journey. The awareness of this fact, the nagging worries of how to find money to meet your obligations and commitments can now usher in a new dimension to your problem - onset of hypertension. Unless you pull yourself together fast and arm yourself with courage and determination, the question of looking for work and money will recede to the background. Your main pre-occupation will be commuting daily between your house and the doctor's clinic.

If you are unfortunate to graduate to this state of health, then you have not got long to enjoy your pension. You will be wise to bring your will up to date, and remember to write in it that your motor vehicle should be sold to pay the balance on your mortgage.

But let us return to the main stream of the misfortune. I earnestly hope that you did not see the 'Daily Sketch' newspaper edition of Monday, 4th September, 1989. There was a news publication in bold letters which would have aggravated your blood pressure and

made you feel more depressed about your present situation:
"MAN HANGS OVER N6,000.

"A retired civil servant said to be in his late 50s has been found hanging in his room at Haruna Street, Okokomaiko, on the outskirts of Lagos at the weekend.

"He was said to have worked in a Federal Ministry before he was retired in 1988. According to the tenants, he had just collected his benefits and thieves broke into his room and stole the N6,000.

"A tenant said that the man had since been crying; he had not been eating he just remained in his room without talking to anybody. He was also overheard saying, "I will kill myself, all the money I laboured for has been stolen..."

But let us again return to your present state of misfortune. What will you do now to keep body and soul together for the rest of your natural life? The question of applying for jobs in response to advertisements is out of it; you are over fifty and no serious organisation takes on a man of over fifty, except, of course, as gateman and watch-night. If you were a University graduate of outstanding academic record, you might find refuge in one of the Universities as a Lecturer. But if you had risen through the ranks in the public service without any appreciable academic background, what occupations could be considered?

By the time you have pondered deeply, especially in the silent hours of the night, you will discover that the following options are open to you:

Secure a political appointment as a member of a Board of a Government Corporation or State-owned company. This, of course, is only feasible or doubtful if you had not been retired on grounds of inefficiency or doubtful probity. How do you set about securing this job? Draw up a list of all the Governors of the different states. Add the names of the President and the Vice-President of the Federation. Now sit back and scan the list, which of them do you know well and who knows you well? If you are fortunate to be on familiar terms with the Governor of your own State, then drive up to the State House one evening and pour out your heart to him. It may, however, be that the Governor who knows you well does not belong to your State. Then, all you have to do is travel there to solicit his help in speaking on your behalf to the Governor of your State.

Should you be fortunate to secure an appointment as a member of a Board or Corporation, always keep at the back of your mind that there are two serious snags in your new job - first, your Board may be dissolved at any moment, even when you have only been there for only two months. You will hear the news of the dissolution on the radio as you sit at table to enjoy your lunch. Despondency grips you again and you lose your appetite. The second snag about this type of job is that being part-time, the remuneration is very small. You will need to occupy yourself gainfully somewhere else, before you can keep your head above water.

A second option open to you is to enter the petty trade of buying and selling - cement, beer, and soft drinks. This is one of the easiest forms of trade which entails little or no complication. Of course, you must be prepared to swallow your pride once in a while to assist in loading the crates and cartons of drink into a van when no helper is available. You must also be prepared for the ordeal of queuing and wrestling with the innumerable women who make this particular trade their exclusive preserve. Of course, you must also take positive steps to be in favour with the Sales Director and Sales Representative of the Companies concerned. What this entails will be clearly manifested to you when after several weeks you do not succeed in getting any allocation of drinks to sell.

Yet another option - Farming. This has become fashionable especially among retired military officers who have unlimited capital to invest. If you approach them for advice on how to go about it all, they will tell you that they took a loan of so many million naira from the bank. You try to follow the advice and go to your bank for a similar loan. You will promptly be chased out of the bank. Dejected and sad, you may have to content yourself with subsistence farming, growing just enough to feed yourself and your family. But this will bring in no money and it is money you are after to balance your personal accounts.

Actually there are numerous possibilities open to you in the way of starting a small business. For example, you can offer to carry the garbage in a few houses, and charge your fees. All you need is a refuse van and some labourers. Or you can become a Horticulturist; grow a collection of flowers and sell them. This requires very little capital; you only need one or two gardeners to keep down the weeds and cultivate the flowers. All you need is a piece of land. Indeed there are endless possibilities.

What about starting a vulcanizing business by the side of the road? All you need is a little boy who is adept at changing tyres. You can sit under the shade and chat with your customers; offer them the day's newspapers to read while their tyres are being patched and inflated; hold them spell-bound with topical discussions on government and politics. In doing so, make sure that you pour a torrent of abuse on the government. This is what the public want to hear. Very soon, your road-side shelter will become a rendezvous for passers-by to stop and air their grievances on the State of the economy, the fall of the naira and on the high cost of living. But let me offer you a word of warning and advice. When you see a man in a French suit, he is an SSO man - secret police state security man. Quickly change your tune; tell your little gathering that the government is doing its very best and all citizens should co-operate with the government to achieve its wonderful programme for the people. Pretend not to notice the state security men.

And finally there is yet one other option to you. Wake up, sit round all day gazing into space, sigh occasionally and bemoan your fate in life. You will not even see the necessity to shave and tidy up yourself daily. When this has been going on for some months, you will begin to feel some dullness inside you, an occasional dizziness and then you will observe that your feet are swollen. When you begin to notice your feet swelling up, you will also observe that a tune begins to hum in your ears. As you listen carefully you will hear the strains of the hymn:

> Man may trouble and distress me,
> It will but drive me to Thy breast;
> Life with trials hard may press me,
> Heaven will bring me sweeter rest.

Once you have persuaded yourself that heaven will bring you sweeter rest, then you can rest your mind and dose away fitfully in your arm-chair while humming

> Nearer my God to Thee
> Nearer to Thee.